Spoons

By Steven Raine

Y'all come back now.

1

Chapter One

Spoons, Nuthook County, South Dakota is, as the Americans would say, 'a one-horse town'; the comments of the horse are not recorded. Back in the day, a hundred or so years ago, the town's jailhouse provided overnight accommodation for drunks, dumped onto the street from Big Molly's saloon. Big Molly's is gone now the jailhouse remains, renamed Spoons Police Department - empty of criminals.

Tanapat and his father were not immediately aware of the man standing quietly by the desk on that hot Wednesday morning. Mr. Mandrake, always polite, waited for a request to state his business, and having established that no invitation was forthcoming, he spoke.

"Good morning, Sergeant. I intend to kill my wife at 2 pm today."

Sergeant Wattana, with a single practiced finger, prodded indifferently at a computer keyboard, inputting numbers from a large stack of traffic citations. He gazed gloomily at the faded photograph on his desk. It was him, a past self in a shiny new police uniform, grinning proudly holding a certificate,

'Sergeant Wattana -Officer of the Year'.

On a chair next to his father, Tanapat, his son, waited for school to begin. Tanapat was playing a game on his cellphone: the most stupid game he had ever seen, he had concluded. On the small phone screen, the animated image of a toilet roll. The objective was to drag his finger over the screen and unroll the toilet paper until the last sheet fell, followed by the message 'Replay or Exit.

"As pointless as my life in this dump," he pondered philosophically.

Every morning, waiting for school to start, Tanapat would be lost in the polluted i-clouds, downloading games that, in better times, he would have considered mind-crushingly stupid. Over the past three years - the time he had lived in the town of Spoons - he had downloaded many of these applications to annoy other people –the 'iPuke' 'iPoop', 'iBurp', 'The Pimple Popper' and 'Jurassic Fart'. He had become an expert with the 'Virtual Electric Razor' app - the 'GPS Toilet Finder' and the 'French Kiss' app - where you practice your kissing technique

Tanapat had recently developed a liking for the detective mystery app, the 'how they did it', 'why they did it' and 'who cares who did it? In this game, the super-villain lives in a volcano, stroking a cat, and has personal control over an orbital death ray satellite.

Tanapat plays the ordinary detective, who just happens to be an indestructible Kung Fu expert with enough guns and knives to invade a small country.

It starts with the dying victim and a short pull-down menu with dialogue like: "Who did this to you?" The victim points a bloody finger at the lampshade, where the first clue is to be found rather than responding with, "Please call me an ambulance."

The victim dies. Witnesses to the murder are unshaven. Male characters in games don't shave, or have mental problems because everyone knows that people with mental problems don't shave.

The lampshade, for reasons not well-explained, has the address of the villain - in code - which the detective has to solve. All accompanied by annoying Techno music.

In the final scene of the game – when you have downloaded an expensive upgrade - the detective will always meet the villain in a dark alley where a screeching cat and a saxophone are playing. The detective pull-down dialogue menu response is, "Cover me". The villain will shout, "Is that all you've got- I'm just getting started."

From nowhere, a gang of Italian-American men wearing white vests, unshaven of course, surround the detective who suddenly finds that his legs are martial arts experts and blood splatters everywhere, especially on the gang's white shirts – Replay or exit – credits - music.

Mr. Mandrake, in the meantime, scanned Sergeant Wattana's disorderly desk.

"Good morning, Sergeant. I intend to kill my wife at 2 pm today."

Tanapat's father gradually became aware of the stranger. Mr. Mandrake beamed an encouraging smile. The Sergeant looked him up and down.

"Are you trying to be funny?" The Sergeant scowled.

Mr. Mandrake reflected. "Not that I am aware."

Tanapat's mouth dropped open when he recognized Mr. Mandrake. His mind flashed 'Replay?' His legs flashed 'Exit'.

Sergeant Wattana became irritated with this unwelcome interruption to his morning routine.

"Threatening to kill your wife is a serious offence, sir!"

Mr. Mandrake smirked. "But I haven't threatened my wife, Sergeant. She doesn't even know I'm here. I have made a statement of criminal intent. It's quite different. You can look it up."

To Sergeant Wattana, this was beginning to sound similar to paperwork, filling in forms. His mind raged against the prospect.

"So, you're going to kill your wife?

He hoped that if he repeated the keywords, he would remember where to find the relevant documents in the Police Department's lawless filing system.

"That is correct," Mr. Mandrake confirmed happily.

"At 2 pm this afternoon?" the Sergeant probed.

"At 2 pm this afternoon," Mr. Mandrake repeated.

The Sergeant remembered some of his early training and the Criminal Psychology classes he had mostly skipped. He spoke in an unconvincing, friendly tone.

"Now, why would you want to kill your wife, sir?"

The reply was prompt.

"Boredom, certainly, and there is a little matter of a 3.8 million-dollar life insurance policy that my wife and I have been paying into for twenty-five years. I am her primary beneficiary, upon her death."

Mr. Mandrake's smile distorted into a wide, confident grin.

Tanapat gawked at Mr. Mandrake and tried to close his mouth. His father finally rose from his chair mostly to an official police height.

"And how exactly, may I ask, are you going to kill your wife if I lock you in a cell all day?"

The question was, of course, expected. "Well, Sergeant, the answer to that is beyond your comprehension. However, I think it is within your son's and his friend's comprehension."

5

Both Sergeant Wattana and Mr. Mandrake twisted their heads, staring at Tanapat, like two hunting dogs focusing on their prey. Tanapat was convinced his jaw had locked wide open forever. His father snapped angrily.

"Do you know this man?"

Tanapat had lost the power of speech.

"It's...It's..."

His phone fell from his sweaty grasp and the toilet roll game flashed its persistent request to be replayed or ended. Sergeant Wattana pitched his head menacingly forward.

"Well?"

Tanapat confessed. "It's...it's... Mr. Mandrake, my English teacher from school!"

His father erupted. "What does he mean, 'it's within your comprehension'? What do you know about this?"

Tanapat uttered a few words, finally allowing his jaw to move. "I dunno what he means. I dunno what he's talking about".

The Sergeant tried to collect his thoughts.

"Go to school...go on...I'll talk to you about this later," he threatened.

Tanapat shot off his chair like an artillery shell but heard his phone vibrating and protesting on the floor. He crawled on his knees, hoping his reduced radar image would make him invisible, before finally grabbing the phone and running out into the street.

The Sergeant now scrutinized the man who was still smiling. Mr. Mandrake calmly sat on the wooden visitors' bench, crossing his legs. The Sergeant opened one of the desk drawers and glanced lovingly down at his gun. He rested one hand on its reassuring, cold, metallic presence and picked up the desk phone with his other hand, pressing a single button.

"Chief, you need to get over here. We've got ourselves a situation."

Chapter Two

Interestingly, the butt is quite rare in nature. Snakes don't have one, dolphins don't need one, and lobsters have lost one. However, priests, presidents, beauty queens, and nuns do have one and fart fourteen times a day, according to the experts on such matters. Indeed, an Indian tribe in South America called the Yanomami, fart as a greeting. In China, you can get a job as a professional fart-smeller. As unpleasant as they no doubt are, one should be grateful that one is not a crinoid, a marine creature with a U-shaped gut and an anus located next to its mouth.

Recommended reading on this fascinating topic is Jim Dawson's 'Who Cut the Cheese: A Cultural History of the Fart', or Shinta Cho's 'The Gas We Pass: The Story of Farts.'

Scientists are a little less certain about whether or not birds can pass gassy buildups from their anus. They point out that birds don't typically carry the same kinds of gas-forming bacteria in their gut as humans to help digest food, so there's nothing to let loose.

It came, therefore, as somewhat of a surprise to the male mallard duck gracefully circling above the tiny town of Spoons in the County of Nuthook, South Dakota, that it couldn't stop farting. A small squeezing sensation, a tight whistling sound, and a gentle rustle of feathers; were the only interruptions to its daily ritual of finding a breakfast beetle. Unknown to the mallard duck, the water it had drunk earlier that morning, from a tin can in the center of town was, in fact, soda water, and the origin of the now alarming amounts of gas accumulating in its ripening intestine.

The large mallard duck, a longtime resident of South Dakota, with its glossy bottle-green head and large grey-brown wings, swooped over Pastor Jack Lovetree's Baptist Church where the emission of its feather fizzler developed into a Satan's Bugle, forcing the hapless creature to make a small adjustment to its flight feathers and consequently its course.

It plunged into a swooping glide down Lakota Street East until another short butt-blast accelerated the duck passed the town's one carpet shop called, pragmatically, 'Carpets People Can Walk On'

The bird flew on by Jed I. Knight's Mini-Mart, before elegantly soaring over the Crazy Horse Bar and Grill, letting out two small pucker-chuckles over the roof of the Mona Pizza restaurant and the Little Big Horn supermarket.

However, the duck's final destination was now in sight, as it spiralled toward Boot Hill Gardens in the centre of town, where it was usually certain of obtaining a meal of pine beetles. The mountain pine beetle eats wood but prefers old wood. The shiny black insect scurried to the best wood in town, a bench in Boot Hill Gardens. It scuttled over the large sign painted on the garden's path: 'No Littering or Peeing' and found the leg of the wooden bench.

Usually, it would have stopped there and gorged itself on the flaking timber, fully aware that it was the subject of intense scrutiny from the clouds. The young pine beetle also knew that further up on the bench was a particularly delicious source of nourishment, for some witty citizen had sliced out a message into the seat with a knife, exposing the tender wood flakes therein. The beetle climbed swiftly and headed straight for the deep, succulent grooves exposed by the carved message which, if beetles could read, would have informed it that,

'This park bench was once Pinocchio.'

First, one large eye and then the other alerted the duck to the presence of breakfast far below. It began its final approach, silent circumferences, targeting the backrest of the bench as the perfect perch from which to launch the attack. It knew that the beetle's eyesight was poor, but it could sense the vibrations of movement and sound.

9

The hungry duck arched and raised its wings as an air-break and floated noiselessly, coming to rest on the top of the bench directly above the feasting beetle. It cautiously gathered and folded its wings so as not to disturb the air, one eye inspecting every movement of the oily-black beetle. It raised one claw ready to plunge into the unsuspecting insect.

An explosion from the mallard's tight anus propelled it forward like a firework; fluttering and flapping tail feathers magnified the thrust as it tried to open its wings to stall the inevitable dive, beak first, onto the bench seat below.

The beetle, which had never sensed such an alarming and terrifying air vibration before, immediately headed for cover. As the duck plunged forward off its perch, it let out a piercing and mournful squawk of frustration.

Chapter Three

Tanapat, eager to escape his wife-murdering English teacher, pushed hard at the glass doors, collapsing into Bruce Springsteen Street. The sun was high and the morning, hotter than a 2-dollar pistol as they say around these parts".

Mr. Mandrake must have gone crazy, "One of those nervous breakdowns teachers like to have all the time," he guessed. At that same moment, he heard an alarming screeching coming from the direction of Boot Hill Gardens. A cry for help from some poor animal in dreadful pain, perhaps. He had no time to investigate. He had to text his friend, Heng,

"OMG! Mandrake!" he typed tantalizingly and trooped across Bruce Springsteen Street.

He tried to put the whole incident to the back of his mind and wait until he could see Heng at school. Maybe his dad and Mr. Mandrake were playing a joke! But that was impossible! His dad had no sense of humour. Still, even with the excitement of the Mandrake mystery, it could not brighten Tanapat's mood, for he had been at Spoons High School for three long, monotonous years and now he was seventeen years old.

He comforted himself with the knowledge that he would soon be free to leave and go back to Thailand. The desire to go home, to Bangkok, filled his dreams. He reflected on the dreary three years he'd spent in the town of Spoons.

At least all the rednecks had stopped calling him Bruce Lee, Bug-Eater, Eggroll, Lemonhead or Ninja. He'd just called them bleach boy or bleach girl. The idiots at school still asked dumb questions. "'Do you eat dogs? Can you do Karate? Can you *speaky English*?"

That was bad enough, but even his friends, back in Bangkok, had started to call him 'Banana', an Asian who had lost his heritage, yellow on the outside, white on the inside.   As Tanapat walked reluctantly to school, he began to remember the time he had first arrived in America. He remembered that to him all white Americans had looked the same. Some had different coloured hair and eyes, "but a pink plastic doll is still a pink plastic doll, no matter what hair you staple to its head or what coloured beads you pop into its eye sockets."

He had come to study in the town of Spoons, Nuthook County, South Dakota, and lived with his dad and stepmom to improve his English. That was the theory.   Unfortunately, the good townsfolk of Spoons didn't speak English or any kind of English recognized in the outside world.

It was hard for Tanapat to think of any job interview where he could say,

"Well butter my butt and call me a biscuit! I can do most any job if y'all give me hard liquor and a hammer."

Or, where he could use words and phrases like,

"'dagnabit' and 'o' yonder'?"

The only useful grammar he'd learned in all that time was, that 'Y'all'' is singular, 'all y'all'' is plural, and 'all y'all's' is plural possessive. Everyone in the town was 'Y'all' and everyone outside town was a nosey, pencil-pushing retard. His stride became ever more sluggish down Main Street, closer to school. He didn't want to be too late, but he never wanted to be early.

The School Principal, Mr. Wyatt Nutter, didn't appreciate 'slackers,'. Tanapat passed by the Spoons Savings and Loan Bank, where Mr. Abner Bracegirdle was the manager. He sniggered; Mr. Bracegirdle was a man of many parts, all of them fat. He passed by the Town Hall and Courthouse, where Mayor Buford Tattersall was both the town Mayor and Judge.

Mayor Tattersall liked to wear a white suit, red waistcoat with a pocket watch. It was his Disneyland interpretation of what the town mayor would wear for the tourists, but tourists never came.

The wife of the mayor, Seraphina Tattersall, according to gossip, never came out from their house. His friend Heng was always up to date with the gossip.

"They do say she is an alcoholic, and crazier than a snake's armpit," his friend Heng would say.

Heng talked this way all the time. Over the last three years, Tanapat had learned that there wasn't much for a judge to do in Spoons. In the whole three years, he had lived in the town, there had only been four trials at the old courthouse. The trial of the man hitting a road sign with a beer bottle, a boy charged with possession of his father's fake driver's license, and the case of a woman who assaulted a dog; enough said about that. The single serious crime was the burning down of a house outside town for insurance, where only the wheels survived.

The only murder trial took place over one hundred years previously when someone got shot in Big Molly's Saloon. The case lasted thirty seconds because the accused man's simple defence was t,

'He needed killin'.

The judge agreed and dismissed the case.

It would be impossible to solve a murder case in Spoons today, Tanapat considered. No one had enough teeth left for a reliable dental record, and years of inbreeding meant that everyone had the same DNA.

The town's laws hadn't changed either. It was still illegal to fall asleep with your shoes on, wear a hat when dancing, or shoot an Indian on horseback from a covered wagon.

Tanapat ambled by the Spotted Elk Laundry, owned by Heng's mom and dad, Mr. and Mrs. Lin. Tanapat yawned.

"It wouldn't be so bad if there was anything to do in this hole," he thought.

"You could see how long you could hold your breath, make anonymous phone calls, burn stuff with a magnifying glass or stare at the back of someone's head until they turned around."

Tanapat missed Thailand!

On a few occasions, he would talk to his friends back home, he would ask them to move the webcam to the window so he could see the sparkling, twinkling city lights of Bangkok. Recently he'd started having the same dream, over and over.

It would begin with the fear and fury of a Bangkok rainstorm, the unexpected flash of lightning sparking and shattering across the tarmac-gray sky.

He would look up into the churning clouds, purple and green, the booming thunder, detonating with anger, his heart punching inside his chest.

He would see the Soi dogs and scrawny cats sharing shelter under cars. Smell the fleshy scents of hot, backpackers, wearing tourist maps as hats diving inside tattoo parlors holding their bottled water.

He'd watch the orange monks taking cover under wild dancing wind chimes. Uniformed car park attendants with whistles damp and silenced.

In the dream, he'd feel the loud spatter, thud, pat, and slap of warm rain on his face, and hear the chime of Buddhist bells in the temple, the call to prayer from the Mosque.

He would run by the busy street stalls with flames and smoke from stir-fried pork, all under the wind-whipped thrashing canopies where old women with painted nails wiped the water from red-skinned lychees.

He watched the boys with thick necks draped in gold chain necklaces, speeding by on mad mopeds, and in this dream, he still felt excited about staying with his dad in the U.S.A. going to an American high school and, perhaps, an American college.

When he awoke, the excitement had gone.

It had been three years ago when his dad had collected him from JFK airport in New York, and they had spent two fantastic weeks driving across America, staying in motels, laughing in Thai. Back then, Tanapat had loved all things American. The Rocky Mountains, the western deserts, the Great Lakes, from the Appalachians to the Mississippi; it was the land of 'what's up?' and 'dude' and 'chill' and 'Twinkies', and free Coca-Cola refills at McDonald's, but best of all there would be no school uniform. There were the great American traditions, chocolate-covered pancakes that looked like animals, drenched in syrup. The American inventions - Batman, Pictionary, Scooby-doo, Texas line-dancing, and peanut butter, although Dr. Pepper still tasted too much like cough syrup for his liking.

"It was me and my dad and a tourist information brochure, driving from New York to South Dakota."

They drove through the parks of New York State where, according to his tour brochure, it was still a crime to walk around on Sundays with an ice cream cone. On to the Hudson Valley mountains and the tall forests of Pennsylvania, where it was unlawful to sleep on top of a refrigerator outdoors or catch fish with any part of your body except the mouth.

They sped down the Interstate in his dad's official police Chevrolet, and it was obvious to Tanapat why the Americans called it 'God's Country'. He remembered the feeling that its beauty could make you cry.

They drove by great ripe farms, high hay barns like cathedrals, and the wheat fields of Ohio, heaving, and rippling like curtains on washday, caught in a summer breeze. Over the Wabash, Tippecanoe Rivers of Indiana, where according to his brochure, no horse is permitted on any street in the city at a speed greater than ten miles per hour, and hotel sheets must be exactly 99 inches long and 81 inches wide.

Then on to the endless flat prairies, the hanging hills over the Mississippi in Illinois, home of the world's largest ketchup bottle, and a jail sentence for anyone giving cats, dogs, or other domesticated animals a lighted cigar. When he turned the page in his travel brochure, dedicated to the State of Iowa, he saw black and white photos of old FBI agents with Tommy guns, blazing away at famous gangsters, John Dillinger, and Charles "Pretty Boy" Floyd. It was still a crime in Iowa for a man with a moustache to kiss a woman in public, and a one-armed piano player must perform for free.

Finally, over the border into South Dakota, cut in half by the Missouri River, home of the Sioux tribe and the Mashed Potato Wrestling Contest, where no horses can enter hotels unless they are wearing trousers.

They had stopped overnight at a motel near the border, next to the 'Turkey Shoot and Bird Sanctuary'. The name of the motel was, 'The Sleep Inn' and underneath a smaller sign: 'Better than a Sofa.'

He remembered the motel lobby where there was a small table. On display, under a glass case, were items left behind by previous guests: a false eye, an artificial leg, a stuffed crocodile, and a handwritten note from the guest in room 12, 'Don't go near the mini fridge-it keeps telling lies, don't believe it.'

For Tanapat the best part of the whole trip was that same evening in a local diner next to the motel. This was the time when he finally dared to ask his dad why he and his mom had gotten divorced back in Thailand or, at least, get his dad's side of the story.

The 'Black Hills Diner' was small, but it was offering a menu special: 'Chang's Chinese Buffet,' a deep-fried, grease-soaked tray of chicken chop suey, egg rolls, chow mein, fake crabmeat stuffed with cream cheese, and, for dessert, fortune cookies. He remembered how he and his dad had laughed out loud because nothing in the buffet was Chinese.

"Do the Americans believe that the Chinese eat this stuff?" he asked his dad in Thai, "where are the rice, vegetables, and meat?"

His dad had not heard the question because he was laughing so much at the little paper message from inside his fortune cookie. 'A day without sunshine is like night.' Tanapat remembered cracking open one of the little pastry packets and reading his message: 'Be nice to friends. You might need them to empty your bedpan when you're old.

His father knew what question Tanapat wanted to ask, and pulled out his wallet retrieving a photograph of Pamela, his American wife, on their wedding day. In the photograph, there was a tall slim woman, with long blonde hair. "To be honest," Tanapat remembered, "all you noticed were breasts". You could probably see them from space."

His father told the not-so-sad story of when he was a policeman in Bangkok. He'd stopped Pamela on a motorbike taxi for a reason he couldn't remember, but he said he couldn't keep his eyes off the woman sitting at the back. He thought her beautiful, she thought him charming.

They arranged to meet at a bar that evening in Siam Square. His dad said that he and Pamela had so much in common. He talked about her a lot in that greasy diner with fake Chinese food. But his father's description still made Tanapat giggle.

"She had lovely lips and a great smile", dad said.

But Tanapat only heard, 'lovely breasts and great breasts.'

Tanapat was 14 years old at the beginning of his American adventure and was still angry about the divorce. His dad had probably concluded that Tanapat was a little too young to understand. Later, when Tanapat finally met Pamela, his dad's new wife, he found she'd gained some weight since the wedding photographs. "OK, a lot of weight!" The long hair was much shorter and the blonde was from a bottle. But she was a nice woman and he had become fond of her over the three years. She was easy to talk to and easy to listen to, and she liked it when he called her Pamela instead of mom. Her conversation was limited. No matter what the question, she would simply repeat, 'You'd better ask your father" or "Wait until your dad gets back" or "Does your father know about that?"

In the morning, on the last day of their journey, Tanapat and his dad were back on the road in the Chevrolet. Spoons, the town, still fifty miles further north, on Interstate 90, close to the city of Sioux Falls, but later Tanapat admitted that it felt three million miles away from his home in Thailand.

The town, as he remembered seeing it for the first time, seemed small, really small, and you didn't need to ask for directions to get around. Not that there was anything to see. He had assumed that Spoons was the same as every other small American town. It was later that he found out that the town was strange even to other Americans. His father's tour of Spoons took about twenty minutes.

"There was Pastor Jack Lovetree's Baptist Church with a sign over the door. 'Honk if you Love Jesus.' Pastor Jack was the priest that had married my father to Pamela's breasts five years earlier."

Next door to the church was the Crazy Horse Bar and Grill, which had a giant neon statue of an old west cowboy that flashed on and off at night. The menu was all-American. You could have a 'rabid dog chiliburger' with two free cans of Budweiser. There was the 'quarter-pound corn dog' the 'double baconator cheeseburger' with extra 'double cheese and mayo' served with a side dish of 'cheese melt with extra cheese'. But, if you wanted a challenge, you could order the 'fire in the hole': a two-foot-long beef hot dog topped with ketchup, yellow mustard, relish, chopped onions, chilli powder, and garnished with triple extra melted cheese.

'It's granny-slappin' good', as the slogan on the takeaway carton claimed.

Crossing Upper Main Street onto Lakota Street East, the carpet shop called 'Carpets People Can Walk On' and next door, the hospital, and Medical Examiner's office.

'Jed I. Knights Mini-Mart' was on the other side of Lakota Street East near Boot Hill Gardens, with its replica Civil War cannon. At the 'Boot Hill Gift Shop ', you can buy small pottery copies of some of the old gravestones in Boot Hill Cemetery.

Tanapat's particular favourites were, 'Here lies Lester Moore, got four slugs from a forty-four.' and 'Here lies Butch, we planted him raw. He was quick on the trigger but slow on the draw.' It didn't matter to Tanapat that they were not genuine but copied from Wikipedia.

The small 'Nugget Trading Post Museum' was owned and managed by the Curator, Mr. Cornfoot, an old white-haired man with thick lens spectacles and a walking stick. He didn't need the walking stick, but he assumed it would help attract the tourists and they would buy more out of sympathy. But the tourists never came.

The museum had a reproduction of an old-west assay office, where the old-time gold prospectors would bring their gold dust to be weighed and valued, complete with reproduction balance scales, a distiller, chemical glassware beakers, funnels, flasks, mortars, and empty bottles labelled 'Nitric Acid'. There was even a little mock-up of a water stream where, according to the sign, 'You can roll up your sleeves, get wet, and harvest real rewards by panning for gold,' but the tourists never came.

Opposite the Nugget Trading Post Museum, was the Mona Pizza, and adjacent was 'Shooz', where you buy shoes." The Mona Pizza was his and his dad's favourite eating place in town. The chef was a big happy man, Arthur Macarthur. He did the cooking while his wife, Magnolia, did the waitressing. "Hi, my name is Magnolia and I will be your waitress for the evening," she would repeat, despite knowing everyone in town for years. The names of the pizzas on the menu always amused Tanapat: 'The Old Smokey' the 'Cheese Me' and the 'Old Folks Pizza' with a thin crust for those who were dentally challenged.

As a special treat, you could order their famous, 'Mr. Beefy' a massive deep pan crust pizza with BBQ bacon chicken, cream cheese, garlic, and parmesan sauce, all topped with grilled sliced banana, fresh red onions, mushrooms, spinach, salted pretzels, balsamic drizzle and, of course, extra cheese.

Next door to the Mona Pizza, was the Little Big Horn Supermarket, owned by the only Native Americans living in Spoons, Mr. and Mrs. Chapawee, affectionately known to all as Chief Running Tab and Shopping Dear.

The Mad General, well, that's what everyone called him, lived on the edge of town in a trailer, on Upper Wounded Knee Road, next to Interstate 90. He called his place an airport because that was where he parked his trailer and helicopter. The Mad General had built the whole helicopter from a kit over many years. He thought, wrongly, it would attract tourists. Tanapat found out people called him 'The Mad General' because when he was young, he had been a pilot in the Vietnam War. But that wasn't quite true. He had spent all his time at the Saigon flying school, learning how to be a pilot. Two days before the end of the war, he got drunk and fell out of the helicopter, breaking his leg in two places. He was speedily shipped back to the U.S.A. so he didn't appear on the war-wounded statistics.

Tanapat checked the time.

Before finally heading down Main Street to Spoons High School on Lakota Street West, there was his weekly ritual to perform and the best view could be had near Boot Hill Gardens. He quickened his pace toward Wounded Knee Avenue. He waited by the Feed Store holding his ear to the air and listening for a clue as to when the event would begin.

The Feed Store was the most popular place in town, because of the January and September hunting seasons in nearby Custer National Park, twenty miles north. This was the time Spoons had a couple of tourists from the nearest big city, Sioux Falls. At those times of the year, you could find half the town's population at the Feed Store.

Between the fifty-pound bags of cattle feed, horse tack, blankets, and bits, below the hanging bridle leathers, and beyond the shelves of vet supplies, rattlesnake, and rabies vaccines, you would find all the town's Bubbas and Billy Bobs who, after dumping their Jolenes and Britneys back home, would head on down to the Feed Store and at the top of their shopping list, a single word: 'Ammo!'" Tanapat had watched every year as the 'good ole boys,' bought 9mm Lugers, Winchester shotguns, NATO semi-automatic rifles, or Navy Seal M60 lightweight machine guns.

Bubba and Billy Bob would leave the Feed Store with the eyes of the Elvis painting following them. Elvis seemed to smile as Bubba and Billy Bob as they banged their heads on the Budweiser beer can wind chime. They did this ritual every year.

Afterwards, it would be time to, 'mosey on up' to the Crazy Horse Fish 'n' Fry campground inside Custer Park, with a pickup truck full of beer and guns and go hunting for Black Hills deer, antelope, and elk. They would get drunk and re-enact the American Civil War's Battle of Gettysburg killing those 'damn Confederate' rabbits or 'damn Yankee Union' rabbits, depending on the colour of the rabbits. Next, a replay of the D-Day landings of World War II against those Nazi squirrels. Their favourite fantasy massacre was the 'mother of all battles' and, 'blowing away them A-Rab, no good towel-head ducks and geese, Y'all.'

Tanapat moved away from the Feed Store and waited in another good spot to catch the weekly action. This was outside the town's newspaper office, 'The Spoons Bugle.' People in shops along Main Street had parted their blinds and curtains awaiting the ceremony. He swiftly remembered why he had stopped reading the town's newspaper 'The Spoons Bugle' one week after he had arrived in town.

"It was a newspaper with no news!"

It had headlines like 'Church candlestick still Missing,' or stories like, 'I'm not dead,' says granny', or 'Is Hitler living in Spoons?"

In the distance, he heard the sound of a motor vehicle.

He was here! It had begun! Old Mr. Rivers was on his way.

Every week, old Mr. Rivers would drive down Main Street. Drunk and mad, fueled on 'Skull Cracker Moonshine Whiskey' which he made himself.

He would ride into town on his sit-down lawn mower with cushioned seats, built-in snow blower attachment, and an 18.5 Horse Power engine, which could accelerate him from 0 to 5 mph in 30 minutes.

He would wave a bottle of moonshine in one hand and grip the driving wheel with the other, as red-faced as a pig with lipstick, whooping, screaming, and shouting, madder than a mule chewing flies!

"He was the Nuthook County Cyborg - half man, half mower, an 86-year-old Terminator."

The old man's lawn mower finally arrived where Tanapat was standing. Its engine fizzled, hissed, and sputtered as the old man also fizzled, hissed, and sputtered and then raised his bottle in a toast to the town, whose name he couldn't quite remember for a few awkward seconds. He squinted at Tanapat, trying to see through a drunken blur, and shouted,

"Hey! You're mighty pretty for a heavy girl."

He drove off down the street singing.

Tanapat watched as he rode off down Main Street.

A large duck flew low, overhead, and Tanapat could have sworn that the bird farted.

Chapter Four

At the top of Mr. Mandrake's 'to-do' list was a two-day stay in the jailhouse. Arrested and charged on Wednesday, a visit from his court-appointed attorney on Thursday, a court hearing and release on Friday, and rich on Monday.

"As prison cells go, it was rather pleasant", Mr. Mandrake had decided. He'd had apartments smaller than this when he was younger, and there was the comforting, familiar odour of toilet disinfectant. But, "it wasn't as if I was going to be there for very long, " he told himself.

The mattress, on the solid bed block next to the yellow-painted wall, had a dark blue rubber cover with a matching pillow. The cell had a tasteful but sterile International Space Station feel about it,

"specially designed for the incontinent hillbilly drunk who liked to mark out his territory with pee, before being thrown back onto the street in the morning", he speculated.

The table was a solid wooden shelf, inserted into the wall, firmly attached with an adjacent stainless steel wall mirror and gleaming clean stainless-steel washbasin, which was next to the toilet with no seat. Nothing was removable or detachable.

No toilet seat made sense to Mr. Mandrake, as he sat down on the toilet to rest. "If there was a cellblock riot in the zoo, there was nothing that could be thrown at the zookeepers."

The steel bars of the door to the cell were an unexpected bonus for Mr. Mandrake. He had been expecting a solid door. "Now I can drag my tin cup across the bars in protest, like the movies; if I had a tin cup, " he thought. More importantly, he could see the clock on the corridor wall through the bars, and time was important to Mr. Mandrake.

Apart from the 'blip-blup, blip-blup' of a dripping tap in the washbasin, everything was perfect, and all was as he had planned.

"The simple-minded Sergeant Wattana," he mused, "Officer-of-the-Year, and his equally half-witted boss, the Police Chief, will both prove predictably stupid. Even now, Sergeant Wattana will be on his way to my house, no doubt practising his counselling skills. He'll take photographs, putting anything he thinks suspicious in little plastic bags like a good little police forensics fan, asking my soon-to-be-ex-wife irrelevant questions.

Sergeant Wattana would follow procedures to the letter", he was counting on that. and would according to Mr. Mandrake's plan, unknowingly be making an important but clumsy contribution to the day's activities. The Police Chief, on the other hand, would be, "phoning the bank and trying to get his life insurance claim stopped. All so predictable".

"I am sure," he thought, "the substantial Abner Bracegirdle, Bank Manager and crook, will tell Sergeant Wattana what I already knew months ago. With a permanent life insurance policy, where the premium has been fully paid for twenty-five years, death proceeds are paid out as a lump sum to the named primary beneficiary - me. The only possible way that payment can be stopped is by the 'Slayer's Rule', well known in the insurance business. That is if the primary beneficiary - me again - were proven to be responsible for the death of the other party named in the policy. That will never be proven. Or, the primary beneficiary, that's me again, were to commit a wrongful act which directly resulted in the death of the other beneficiary. That will also never be proven. Then, payment can only be stopped if there are ongoing criminal proceedings, which there will not be."

Mandrake had thought of everything and relaxed on the bed. He pulled the rubber pillow under his head and, looking through the bars, checked the clock on the corridor wall.

"Soon, I would be charged officially, under the South Dakota laws dealing with statements of criminal intent."

Mr. Mandrake had studied that law very carefully.

"Now, let's see. How does it go? 'That I did, knowingly, purposely, recklessly, maliciously and wilfully, on this day, make a statement of criminal intent, and the simple-minded Sergeant and his not-so-dumb son, Tanapat, had witnessed the aforementioned statement.' I will also have the right to remain silent, not to make a formal statement, not to answer questions, or be made to take a lie detector test, unless by consent and with my lawyer present, blah, blah, blah. I will, of course, waive my right to trial, plead guilty, be sentenced at Friday's arraignment hearing, first offence, no previous convictions, maximum fine, two thousand dollars, case closed, go to the bank, without passing 'Go'- collect 3.6 million dollars.

The underpaid but no doubt ambitious State's Prosecution Attorney, having been dragged in from Sioux Falls and his golf game, will try to upgrade the charge from 'Criminal Intention' to 'Criminal Threat'. He will cite 'People versus Moore, 1966', and attempt, unsuccessfully, to establish that the defendant- that's me- acted with the specific intent to deprive the true owner- my wife- of her property- and deprive her of her useless, pointless life.

My own equally underpaid Defence Attorney, also from the Sioux Falls golf course, will, with my help, object, pointing out that in law it can only be a threat if the person threatened knew of the threat beforehand, which my wife did not. Or, if she was in reasonable fear of me doing her criminal harm, which isn't reasonable, as I will be locked up in the slammer at the same time my wife will lay down her last knitting needle. Therefore, we respectfully submit, Your Honor, that a conditional threat is not a criminal threat in law: 'People versus Mendoza 1997', 'People versus Lopez 1999', and now 'People versus Mandrake', objection sustained, case closed."

Chapter Five

Mr. Mandrake fondly recalled the time he had first decided to,

"...bump off the old bag".

It was six months ago in his classroom after school marking homework.

He hated marking homework.

"My students are a depressing reminder that there must be something fundamentally wrong with the Theory of Evolution.

He remembered marking the final grubby, grease-stained book. The title of the masterpiece was:

'My Dad the Zombie' by Delmont Spukler

Mr. Mandrake drew a deep breath and remembered the story:

'My dad was trying to kill me. At first, I couldn't tell the difference. My dad was always chasing me around with power tools, but then I saw his eyes. They were red and shining like two red marbles that someone had dropped in spit and then held up to the light. His mouth was full of blood, like a tube of toothpaste, where all the toothpaste had been taken out and replaced with red stuff. I felt an emotion that had no name. Well, there's probably a name for it, but I don't speak Latin. It walked down the stairs toward me, looking much like something no one had ever seen before. It picked up a chair that wasn't usually on the stairs and then threw it at me. The chair missed me, but it didn't miss me. I was angry like when you can't turn off the Windows screensaver. The chair hit my leg and I couldn't move. It hurts like when you staple your tongue to your lip. He kept walking down the stairs like whatever, and because he wasn't my dad anymore, he didn't notice the bowling ball.

He tripped and tumbled like underpants in a washing machine and then just lay there like an object not moving. I was like really scared. It was the kind of scared that nobody knows the name for, like those little plastic things that close sandwich bags; nobody knows what they're called, either. It wasn't my dad anymore. He was some man I didn't know like those dudes at the end of the movie credits called something like 'second bad guy.' Then I woke up because it was all a dream. Please don't give me an 'F' again Mr. Mandrake my dad will kill me for real.'

Mr. Mandrake was a disappointed man. He'd been a disappointed young man, a disappointed middle-aged man and now he was a disappointed old man. He'd worked at Spoons High School for thirty years. That wasn't to say that in all that time he hadn't learned anything useful from watching his students over those many years.

Watching kids play, he'd learned that cats throw up twice their body weight when thrown like a football. Chewing gum and computers are not compatible. Children will only read newspapers if there are reports of ten murders, two electrocutions, and at least one demonic possession. One child's voice is louder than two hundred adults in a crowded room; one child's bacteria are one thousand times more infectious than any adult. Books do not bring wisdom unless you stand on four of them to hit the students when they walk past. On the positive side, a cup full of perfectly sharpened pencils on the desk is a thing of beauty.

He recollected that after marking the books, he'd gone back to the school office for some reason he couldn't quite remember, habit probably. He had seen the memo on the school secretary's desk, the plan for his retirement ceremony, a modest affair. There was to be an announcement at the assembly. The students would clap, like bored spectators at a 0-0 three-hour basketball game. Then he would get a cheap brass clock, an insulting reference to the passage of time, and be expected to suffer long retirement days watching daytime television or developing new interests like how to keep breathing.

"There was, also, my wife." He shuddered.

Mr. Mandrake had gone home early from school that day and had sat in the pristine, brushed, scrubbed, and vacuumed the living room.

"My wife," he remembered, "had her back to me and was bending down over the coffee table."

She was spraying furniture polish. A lemon-scented cloud hovered around her head. He looked at her bottom - it was difficult to avoid, as it now obscured most of the light from the window.

He could not even remember why he had married the old hag, thirty-five years ago.

'Dearly beloved, we are gathered here in the presence of God- to witness the death of this man in Holy Matrimony. Wilt thou have this woman to be thy lifetime tormentor; to keep her, feed her, and buy fashion accessories? And wilt thou, the elephant in a wedding dress, place this dog lead and collar, around thy husband's neck and repeat after me: I thee wed, in sickness and in health; to take all, from this day forward. I now declare you slave and mistress.

On that day, Mr. Mandrake could think of nothing but his living death in retirement. He thought of his "wife's massive butt sucking the light and oxygen out of his retirement". He thought of the twenty-five-year-old, fully paid-up life insurance policy that would be worth, he had estimated, 3.6 million dollars.

"She was old, ugly, and stupid! She had to go! But how to knock off the old cow."

He wanted to be free. He wanted to live! He wanted to sit on a beach in Tahiti and annoy waiters in restaurants. Why couldn't he have some life, liberty, and the pursuit of happiness? He remembered.

He remembered the vision of his wife flopping back into her favourite armchair and pulling out her knitting. On that day it had been all too clear to him, that the old woman had no intention of leaving Planet Earth any time soon.

"Old she might be but she was as healthy as a bull. She would need some assistance 'till death do us part', and a little encouragement to pass over to the great knitting pattern in the sky. How could it be done? Roller-skates? What about roller skates on the stairs? Oh dear, how did they get there? Some people can be so clumsy...... No, not very realistic. Rat poison, yes, he could put it in her coffee. Would you like more sugar in your rat poison dear? How about a car accident, but the old hag never drove the car more than 5 mph. No one would ever believe she accidentally swerved off a cliff at 5mph.

But, Officer...I came home from work and she had hung herself from the light fitting. Impossible! No light fitting could support that weight.

Officer, I came home from work and she had fallen on her knitting needles. No, but amusing"

Officer, she attacked me with a knitting needle. It was only self-defence when I hacked her to death with that axe I had in the living room and buried the pieces in the back garden...No, too many questions."

It was then he realized, there was always hunting season. Maybe he could tell her they had both been invited to a fancy-dress party, at the Fish 'N Fry Campground near Custer National Park. He would have to think of a hunting theme, a costume idea for the party...

"Yes, that Walt Disney cartoon film, 'Bambi', she could go as, let me think, yes, as Thumper, the annoying rabbit. She would enjoy knitting the costume."

I would make sure she had too much to drink, and drive slowly so it took a long time. She would certainly want to relieve herself eventually.   Leave her in the park and let the rednecks shoot her. The 'Good ole boys' would be far too drunk to question why a fat, talking five-and-a-half-foot rabbit was running around the woods."

He recalled how his wife, with some ceremony, eventually placed her knitting down on the arm of the chair and stood.

'I am going to the toilet.' she had announced as though it were some great adventure.

It was always the same routine - flush, pause; squeeze, pause, bleach squirt, pause, and flush, the same toilet performance every day.

That was when Mr. Mandrake first had the idea!

He'd had the idea of killing his wife for at least thirty out of the thirty-five years of their marriage, but his retirement had lent some urgency to the issue.

He knew she was a woman of fixed routines, doing the same things, at the same times, in the same ways. Maybe that was the key! She had smiled at him and continued her knitting.   He remembered hearing the Mad General's helicopter buzzing over the town.   He looked up at the living room ceiling.

The sound of the helicopter outside, the knitting, the toilet, the living room ceiling fan spinning slowing around and around...her fat butt,"

All these thoughts, once so annoying and disconnected, had begun to come together in his mind.

That was six months ago and ever since that time, Mr. Mandrake had followed her every move, an attentive and dedicated student in the school of murderous intent, with only one subject on the curriculum.

"How to kill the old bag and get away with it."

Chapter Six

Tanapat was early for school. He mounted the steps into the large entrance hallway, where most students gathered before lessons. Spoons High School was on the edge of town, a concrete block built in the 1950s when concrete was cool. He guessed that the windows were small so the cost of eventually putting in steel bars would be less. According to Tanapat's research on the 'Yippy' search engine, the school had been built at a time when men were real men, women were vacuum cleaner attachments, and children did say, 'Gee Whizz'. In those days, girls were known as babes, boys were cool cats and if you weren't a hip daddy-o you were, 'cruisin' for a bruisin' from a 'knuckle sandwich

Happy days.'

He always liked to check out the school notice boards on the far wall to see if there was anything new, and to avoid eye contact with his enemies. The section of the notice board with the title Hall of Fame was reserved for the famous and honoured alumni from Spoons High School, empty of course. Next were the fire safety instructions: 'in case of fire, line up quietly in single file from the smallest to the tallest.' He'd always assumed this must mean tall people burn slower than short people.

He noted Principal Nutter had added some new school rules to the already extensive list. In between 'No Cellphones in Class' and 'Don't make animal noises at the female teachers,' new notices were added, 'A doctor's note is required to use hand sanitiser', 'No burping in class' or 'kneeling on frozen peas', the younger students had recently discovered this as a cheap alternative to a leg tattoo.

He continued reading. 'Do not eat lunch off the floor.' 'You are not allowed to bring your own ketchup' and 'An empty bottle is not a toilet.' Next to the 'Hall of Fame' was the more complete 'Hall of Shame', names of students who had earned in-school detentions that week.

The names were the same every week: Jim Bob, Billy Ray Pickett, Kyle Elwood, and Jolene Delmont. Tanapat read the several small pieces of paper pinned to the board informing students of new after-school clubs, organized by vindictive teachers, who had to offer an extra-curricular activity but didn't want anyone to attend. 'How to make a balloon-animal club,' 'How to make a snow-globe club,' 'How to photograph a puppy properly club,' and, 'How to think of a password other than 'password' club.'

Under 'Special Announcements' was news of the Spoons High School basketball team, The Titans, reaching the quarterfinals along with Deadwood High, and the playoff would be in the town of Deadwood. The school trip, this semester, was to be yet another 'field trip' to the old abandoned paper mill outside town, supervised by Mr. Mandrake, again.

The school canteen, 'I Am a Snack Bar, Eat Me,' displayed the same menu on the notice board. Customers still alive could order 'The Mega,' which was a beef and potato cheeseburger or egg and cheddar breadsticks with BBQ buffalo chicken and cheddar. The chef's special was the 'Hot Hawaiian Ham-and-Cheddar-with-Chicken Pizza' or a potato and cheese salad with beef and potato burritos. The dessert menu included peanut butter chocolate cheesecake with extra chocolate chip cookies, or, 'Custard's Last Stand,' a chocolate cheesecake with custard.

Tanapat could feel his friend behind him and he turned to look at this apparition,

"Oh my God, what are you wearing, Heng?"

Heng was wearing LeBron performance basketball shoes, chino camel pants, and a Fung Brothers T-shirt. His hair was held high on his head by an oil slick of gel and combed over to the right with a parting on the left. On his back was a multi-coloured Hershel backpack, and he was holding a Snapback cap in one hand with sunglasses in the other.

"Swaggy init?" Heng grinned. "Be the best version of yourself, you feel me, Bro?"

Tanapat reluctantly replied, "I feel you."

"Why yo' wear that old jacket every day, bro? I always see you in that rag dude!" Heng snorted, pulling at the sleeves of Tanapat's jacket.

Tanapat hadn't noticed what he wore every day and cared even less. "It has pockets to keep my stuff in," he explained inadequately.

Huang Lin was Tanapat's only friend in school. He was Chinese-American and his parents, Mr. and Mrs. Lin, owned the Spotted Elk Laundry. Tanapat had once asked why a Chinese laundry had the name 'Spotted Elk.'

Heng had said, "There are levels to this 'ting. We ain't 'bout that life. We steppin' up the game, ya dig?"

Tanapat, understandably, never asked again.

Huang Lin's nickname was Heng and he was always desperate to fit in and become one of the 'bleach boys'. Tanapat was known to Heng by the nickname, 'Boss.'

"What's happening, Boss, dude? Got yo text?" Heng said in an exaggerated and ludicrous West Coast accent.

"Mr. Mandrake is with my dad. He says he's going to kill his wife!" Tanapat whispered.

Heng was shocked. "NO WAY!" Heng shouted.

"Heng, I wish you would stop talking like that!" he snapped.

Tanapat could now see the enemy over Heng's shoulder. This was the reception committee and they were waiting at the end of the hallway, blocking the way through to the classrooms. They were giggling, pointing, and talking in a huddle like hyenas waiting for a wounded wildebeest to fall behind the main herd.

Tanapat recalled how the small gang had first tormented Heng, and then himself from his first days in the school, calling themselves the 'Spell Checkers', but nobody knew why. The entire population of the school had taken five seconds to rename the gang the 'Small Peckers'.

The leader was Jim Bob who liked to be called P. Diddy. There was Billy Ray Pickett, aka. Mr. Mumbles, because he hardly ever spoke, and Kyle Elwood, or 'Big Drizzle', named because he was always wiping snot on his sleeve.

The only girl in the gang was, Jolene Delmont, nicknamed Roadkill, with bleached blonde hair and a picture of a diamond wedding ring tattooed on her finger.

"She was as sexy as a goat in socks." Heng had judged.

It was clear to Tanapat, that Jim Bob was to be the nominated tormentor for the morning, having "...borrowed the gang's remaining brain cell for the purpose."

Heng was the first to notice Jim Bob moving forward from the pack.

"Lookout, he's loaded up on loudmouth soup," Heng whispered.

Tanapat rolled his eyes. "Shut up, Heng."

By common agreement, Jim Bob was the most stupid in the gang, but all things are relative.

The only conversation Tanapat ever remembered having with Jim Bob had revealed his lack of knowledge about anything outside Spoons and was based on computer games and bad movies. To Jim Bob, all Russians were communist spies; the French didn't speak English and hated tourists, especially the British. The British had bad teeth and hated tourists, especially the French. The Germans ate sausages and wanted to take over the world. The Arabs were terrorists who married belly dancers. The Greeks were lazy, olive-munching hairballs. The Africans were poor, hungry, jungle dudes. The Indians walked over fire pits with needles through their mouths. The Chinese were short and wore glasses. The Japanese were short, wore glasses, and ate raw fish. The Filipinos liked kidnapping foreigners, soap operas, karaoke, and shoes. The Vietnamese wore funny hats and slept in rice fields, and as for the Thais: they had a funny language and worked in massage parlors. All the men were ladyboys but prettier than the girls.

Jim Bob now placed himself forward from the rest and shouted across the hall. "Hey, Ching-Chong!" What do you call an Asian in a school? The Janitor!" The Spell Checkers erupted into exaggerated laughter, giving each other high fives.

Heng whispered in Tanapat's ear,

"Man, that boy's dumb! The wheel is spinning, but the hamster is dead."

Jim Bob heard the comment, "Yeah! Yeah! If I'm so dumb, why do all Asians work in 7-11s?" Jim Bob nodded as though he had said something astoundingly clever.

"Because we own them all!" Tanapat calmly replied.

All students in the hall, apart from the Spell Checkers, giggled.

Heng stood behind Tanapat and shouted back at Jim Bob. "If stupid could fly, you'd be a jet, bleach boy." Jim Bob didn't understand what it meant but a shark could only move forward, and he started to run at Heng. Tanapat stood between Heng and Jim Bob.

The gang all shouted. "Whoop his ass, P. Diddy!"

Jim Bob and Heng were face-to-face, with Tanapat in the middle. Heng started first.

"Hey, Snow White, let's see what yo' about, we gonna eat you up and spit you out."

"Ayeeeee…" All the students shouted together.

Jim Bob thought for a second.

"Yo, Bruce Lee bug-eater, better start prayin', gonna mash yo up, know what I'm sayin'?"

The rest of the students started to sway and dance. Heng waved his head from side to side.

"You think yo cool, from the hood, but yo a dumbass peckerwood. Get back to yo trailer, yo redneck flunkey, I ain't speakin' to no albino monkey.

"Ayeeeee…" The hall shouted back enthusiastically.

Jim Bob's freckled face turned redder.

"Better watch out who you diss, your mama ain't here to kiss you. You better run, gonna end up dead, lookin' to crack me open a lemon head."

"Ayeeeee…" The hall yelled louder.

Jim Bob jutted out his chin back and forth.

"I smack you up like I was your daddy. Kick yo butt back dat rice paddy."

"Ayeeeee…" The hall screamed.

Jim Bob was much bigger than Tanapat and towered over him, waving his arms about wildly like an agitated chimpanzee.

Jim Bob had assumed waving your arms about wildly like an agitated chimpanzee, was what gang leaders did in these situations.

Jim Bob tried to manoeuvre around Tanapat to get to Heng.

"Out of the way, ladyboy or yo gonna use that fancy Thai boxing?"

Tanapat looked about to see if any teachers were near, then brought his knee up swiftly into Jim Bob's groin.

Jim Bob's eyes bulged, his red freckled face went beetroot red, his cheeks inflated like a bull-frog and he let out a gust of breath like a deflating Whoopee Cushion, crumpling in agony to the floor, holding his groin.

All the girls laughed, and all the boys went silent.

Tanapat now towered over Jim Bob.

"I don't know anything about Thai boxing, will that do? Y'all have a nice day now."

Tanapat remembered three years ago he would have never dreamed of doing anything like that, but three years in this place had changed him.

"You get tired of being scared all the time," he had explained to Heng.

"Being frightened every day is exhausting and there comes a time when you say, to hell with it! Sink or swim, live or die."

Tanapat was now Heng's hero. Heng waved a fist at Jim Bob, first making sure he was behind Tanapat. "Yeah, bleach boy, if you climb in the saddle, be ready for the ride."

Tanapat pushed Heng to the other side of the hall and held a hand over his mouth in an attempt to silence him. Heng gave a muffled shout.

"You bleach boys couldn't hit the ground if you fell twice!"

Principal Nutter's voice boomed and echoed across the hall.

"WHAT'S ALL THIS NOISE?"

Tanapat had noticed over three years, no matter what the situation, Principal Nutter always said, "What's all this noise." He would change the volume depending on the situation.

Jim Bob pointed an accusing finger at Tanapat as he struggled painfully to rise from the floor.

Tanapat shrugged and smiled.

Principal Nutter thundered.

"GET TO YOUR CLASSES, NOW!"

Chapter Seven

The Mandrake residence, a house without wheels, was in a neat suburb built on the old site of a farm called Cobbler's Knob. Sergeant Wattana drove his blue and white striped Chevrolet leisurely down Rivington Avenue, looking for number ten. He had orders to talk to Mrs. Mandrake, take photographs and get permission to search for anything suspicious inside or outside the premises. He was to stay with Mrs. Mandrake until after 2 pm.

He found the Mandrake house and pulled over, his heart pounding. All was calm and quiet with a freshly cut lawn, neat flowerbeds, and the Mandrake's Nissan in the driveway.

"What do I say, what do I tell her?" He desperately tried to rehearse something.

"Good morning, Mrs. Mandrake, your husband wants to kill you.

No! No! She would just say, 'We've been married for thirty-five years; don't you think I know already?"

"How about, Good morning, Mrs. Mandrake, I'm afraid I have some bad news. No, it would frighten her to death. She'd scream like a pig on fire."

"Good morning, Mrs. Mandrake, good news, you're still alive."

"Good morning, Mrs. Mandrake, I'm conducting a survey."

"Mrs. Mandrake, did you know your hair and fingernails continue to grow after death?"

Sergeant Wattana was now desperate.

The truth was he had never done anything like this before, and he didn't know what to say. It was time to get some advice. He clicked open the glove compartment. Immediately there was a cascade of objects falling to the floor, three spoons, one sock, spare bullets, a rubber dinosaur, and a hardboiled egg. To his surprise, he also found a pair of gloves. He'd never seen gloves in a glove compartment before. He searched through the books, leaflets, and magazines.

He made a mental note of all the publications he had not had time to read:

'So you want to buy a Miniature Donkey'

'It's No Sin to be Fat',

'The Devil Made Me Do It',

and 'Practical Witchcraft'.

He finally found what he was looking for: a small booklet entitled, 'Police Department Counseling Skills Handbook: Four easy stages to make the client feel relaxed'. He read the summary at the back optimistically.

'Stage one: Body Language. Remember to always smile, lean forward, make eye contact, and nod to convey your interest.

Stage two: Activating the Event. Encourage the client with short, gentle prompts, "uh-huh," "really?", "tell me more," etc.

Stage three: Empathy. Place yourself in the client's situation.

Stage four: The Miracle. Ask the client to imagine they are very tired. During the night, a miracle happens and all the problems are solved.'

Sergeant Wattana closed the small booklet with new confidence and placed it on the seat next to him.

"Well, it all seems simple enough," he thought to himself.

He imagined how the scenario would play out.

"Mrs. Mandrake would be in the kitchen washing the breakfast cups and plates. There would be a knock at the door. She would hastily dry her hands on a towel, check her hair in the mirror and go to the front door. She would ease the door open slowly. She would see me, smiling, leaning towards her in the doorway and staring directly into her eyes. That's when I nod my head."

"Why am I here Mrs. Mandrake?"

"How the hell do I know?" She steps back.

"Uh-huh, I see, I see."

"What do you want?"

"Uh-huh, uh-huh, tell me about it"

"Get away from me!"

"How do you feel Mrs. Mandrake?"

"Get your feet off my doorstep!"

"Uh-huh, uh-huh, tell me more,"

"Are you mad? What the hell are you talking about?"

She kicks at my foot holding the door open.

"I feel your pain, uh-huh"

"Get away or I'll call the police! Someone help me!"

"You want to go to bed, there will be a miracle."

Mrs. Mandrake screams.

Sergeant Wattana woke from his counselling skills daymare. He started to beat his head on the steering wheel.

Chapter Eight

"Teachers always get it wrong." Tanapat had once observed. "If I don't answer their question, it doesn't mean I don't know the answer. The teacher's 'fun' lesson is never fun. The teacher's, 'interesting fact' is never interesting, and there is no way any of us will ever divide into small discussion groups, elect a group leader, take notes, and vote on the most important topic."

When Mr. Bunsby, the History teacher, finally faced up to this reality, his class became like all the other lessons at Spoons High School, 'death by PowerPoint' full of neon yellow fonts and smiley faces. Or as Heng would say,

"There's no cheese on that teacher's cracker!"

Tanapat liked the history class on Wednesday morning; not because he learned anything but because the lessons were just funny. He remembered his first history class about the brave settlers arriving in America, escaping religious intolerance. The neon yellow fonts and smileys told the tale of the first settlers travelling over the wide Atlantic in a tiny wooden sailing ship called the 'Mayflower', establishing religious freedom, taming the wilderness, and hacking their way through thick dark forests, while the same time fighting off thousands of savage natives. The Pilgrim Fathers had celebrated their triumph with a Thanksgiving Feast in 1621 - and every year thereafter,

or so the PowerPoint claimed.

Tanapat frowned as he reminded himself that in most of Mr. Bunsby's History lessons, the truth was never allowed to mess up a PowerPoint. Tanapat had discovered, with just three mouse clicks an alternative, but more believable, version of Mr. Bunsby's heroic epic of settlers and rampaging Indians.

"Put another way, as they say around these parts, 'Puttin' yer boots in the oven don't make 'em bread.''

It seems the brave settlers had not first travelled west from England to the New World, but east to Holland. There they had lived in the town of Leiden for over two years and would have stayed if they could have found jobs and if their children had not started to lose their ability to speak English, and had not begun to curse, swear and get drunk with the locals. Only then, did the Pilgrims make the journey to America, mainly to protect their children from these ungodly influences.

Their version of 'religious freedom', once arrived in the New World, meant that Catholics, Jews, Christians, and anybody else who was not a Puritan was immediately outlawed from the colony.

The Native Americans didn't need to kill the settlers; they just sat back and laughed as the Pilgrims spent the first harvest season digging holes looking for gold, and in their spare time hanging each other for blasphemy. As for taming the wilderness, well, the idea that the Native Americans had lived in harmony and worshipped Mother Earth, Father Moon, Brother Coyote, and Sister Raccoon may not have been strictly accurate either.

Native Americans had spent thousands of years clearing the land and cutting down the forests. The settlers, far from being outnumbered by the warlike natives, failed to realize that plagues and famine had killed ninety per cent of the Native American population before they had even arrived.

Later in the semester, the 'Old American West' was to be the topic of a PowerPoint with little pictures of bullet holes serving as bullet points, complete with an animated cowboy, who fired his revolver whenever the slides changed.

Mr. Bunsby described the Old West as,

"a time when men were men, and women were as well. It was a time when brave American cowboys protected innocent families from being massacred by savages. It was the lawless frontier, with quick-draw shoot-outs, bank robberies, sheriffs, and Native Americans all happily murdering each other."

Heng had got it about right when he said after that class,

"Well knock me down and steal my teeth. He got the facts as messed up as a kite in a hail storm!"

Tanapat remembered he had gotten an 'F' grade from Mr. Bunsby because his essay was different from the official PowerPoint. Tanapat's essay on the topic reported that 'most of the original cowboys were Mexican and not American, and the Native Americans weren't mindless zombies, killing anything that moved. Few settlers died in so-called Indian attacks. In the real history of the old west, farmers were more likely to be accidentally trampled to death by their own cows. In the forty years from 1850 to 1890, there were about twelve bank robberies, compared to six thousand bank robberies in one day in the modern U.S.A. Today's America would have made Jesse James and Billy the Kid run 'faster than green grass through a goose.'

It took Mr.Bunsby a whole semester to finally get around to the history of Spoons, but Tanapat had done his homework.

"It turns out..." Tanapat informed Heng, who didn't even attempt to pretend any interest,

"...that the land where the town of Spoons now stands was stolen from the Lakota Indians in the 1870s because of the discovery of gold in the nearby Black Hills, South Dakota.

The town of Spoons was famous for…, well, nothing. None of the famous characters of the day - Billy the Kid, Buffalo Bill, Butch Cassidy, Calamity Jane, Doc Holliday, Deadwood Dick, Jesse James, and Wyatt Earp - ever came anywhere near Spoons, most likely because they didn't know where it was, and cared even less.

Neither did the railroad ever come to the town. Spoons had managed to be ignored by all the great events and people in American History."

Back in the day, the town of Spoons had three places you could go: - Big Molly's Saloon, the Jailhouse, and Boot Hill Cemetery, in that order, usually. You got robbed and killed in the first and second and then buried in the third. Even ten years after the town had been established there was only a population of ten, a living population, that is. The town was surrounded by 60,000 Native Americans from nine different tribes – all of the Dakota, Lakota, and Nakota tribes which made up the Sioux Nation. The only recorded confrontation between the Sioux and the town was when facing the threat of starvation, a group of Dakota Sioux planned to attack the good folks of Spoons until the Sioux realized that the citizens were poorer and more hungry than they were.

Legend has it that the Sioux started leaving food for the townsfolk, every month for a whole year, in exchange for metal spoons.

Metal spoons of all shapes and sizes fascinated the Dakota Sioux. They would leave food for the townsfolk and the townsfolk would leave them spoons. This is how the town got its name. It seems the town had no recorded name before.

In 1889, South Dakota was separated from North Dakota and became the 40th State in the United States of America, but the town of Spoons didn't appear on any map until 1922, and even then you needed a microscope to find it.

Unfortunately, for the good citizens of Spoons, someone at the Tax Office in Washington did have a microscope. In 1922 there was a small ceremony in the half-built Town Hall where the government of the United States officially recognized the town, a small band played and the citizens were handed a bill for all unpaid taxes from 1870.

The history of the United States continued to roll right on by the little town. The First World War had been over for two years before the citizens even knew there had been a war. They eventually found out because a page from the 'Sioux Falls Times' had drifted into town on the wind. In the Second World War, no citizens of Spoons were invited to enlist, and certainly none of its citizens felt an urgent need to volunteer."

The Wednesday morning PowerPoint had already enthralled half the class into a coma. Today's offering from Mr. Bunsby was his fairy tale about General George Armstrong Custer's courageous 'last stand' against thousands of savage, flesh-eating Indian zombies at the Battle of the Little Big Horn. But, Tanapat wasn't paying too much attention.

He and Heng were patiently waiting for Mr. Mandrake's English class to begin later that day.

Chapter Nine

After about five minutes the pain from Sergeant Wattana's forehead was greater than his fear of confronting Mrs. Mandrake at her front door. He finally found the courage to 'walk the walk to talk the talk', or at least knock on the door. He had his camera, his gloves, and several small plastic bags and containers for comfort. He checked that his 'handle-talkie' duplex radio was working, and tuned it to the frequency of the dispatcher back at the Police Department. The dispatcher console had acknowledged his message, '10-41-Arrived on the scene, all was 10-4'.The police jargon reassured him.

He stopped in front of the Mandrakes' door, took a deep breath, and knocked. There was a pause. He could hear sounds on the other side, the noise of zips pulling, an animal growling and grunting. Without warning, the door flew open. A beast that looked like a large ape was pointing some kind of weapon at him and lunging forward.

"Jesus Christ!" he shouted, forgetting he was Buddhist, he stumbled back a few steps, drew his gun, and held it with both shaking hands. He aimed at the beast.

"Put the...the..." He narrowed his eyes to get a closer look at the weapon the ape thing was holding.

"Put the...uh... ray gun down please, and step away."

"NOOK-NECK –PAH-TAK," it shouted.

He had no idea what it meant, but it didn't sound like, 'Have you had breakfast?'

"Where is Mrs. Mandrake?" Sergeant Wattana demanded to know.

"What do you want, HU-MAN?" it growled.

51

He looked a little closer at the being. It was wearing something resembling black jeans and a kind of leather biker's jacket with metal stripes along each sleeve. There was a series of metallic panels, starting from the back of the neck which ran over each shoulder, like armor. They reminded him of the vinyl table placemats from the Mona Pizza restaurant, attached to the jacket by small hooks.

It wore a huge black belt with a metal belt buckle. Over its left shoulder, to the waist, was a rough, thick sash. He was sure it was an old firefighters' hose, cut open and flattened, interwoven with chain links. On its feet, it wore high-top boots, biker boots with metallic strips around the soles. The top of the boots was encircled with small horns, similar to steel coat hooks. It wore fingerless gloves with black claws.

By far the strangest sight was its head. It was bald with what looked like the skeleton of a dead animal attached to its skull, and bony ridges worn like a hat. On either side of these ridges, were long braided locks of shoulder-length brown hair. Its nose also had small ridges to the forehead. The appearance of the beast seemed somehow familiar.

"My God! You're a Klingon from Star Trek."

Sergeant Wattana lowered his gun.

"HEGHLU-MEH- CAC- JAJVAM. Today is a good day to die, HU-MAN," it announced.

He stammered. "Mrs. Mandrake, is…is that you?"

"My name is Lursa, a commander in the Klingon Empire," she insisted in a deep guttural, rasping tone.

"Right!" The only response he could make.

Mrs. Mandrake peeled off the latex mask and removed the wig. Underneath was the rather ordinary face of a woman in her sixties.

"It's not a ray gun," she protested indignantly.

"It's a replica 'Klingon Disruptor'. It's the officially licensed Star Trek collectable, expensive, and very rare. It only needs two triple 'A' batteries."

"You frightened me to death, Mrs. Mandrake!" He managed a grin.

"Excellent! I am determined to win a prize, this time, at the Trek convention."

So, Mrs. Mandrake was a 'Trekkie' he realized, not knowing whether this would make his job easier or harder.

"I don't have long!" she insisted, ushering him into the house and looking to see if the neighbours were watching. Sergeant Wattana wondered if she already knew why he was there and if that was why she had said she didn't have long.

"You'll have to be quick. I must take the shuttle to the planet for more supplies."

"What?"

"Take the car to town and do some shopping," she translated impatiently.

He had already decided that he couldn't allow her to do that, but the immediate objective was to get her full attention. She pushed him gently towards the living room. "Would you like me to replicate you a beverage? Blood wine or coffee?"

"Nothing for me, thank you," he said unintelligently.

"I will have to change, please..." She gestured towards the living room and climbed the stairs, swearing in Klingon, "HU-MAN - D'BLOK-BAKTAG!"

Sergeant Wattana made sure his camera was charged and started to take pictures of everything in the living room.

On the mantelpiece, next to the model of 'Star Trek's Enterprise, was a small plaster figurine of Yoda from 'Star Wars'. On the wall above was a piece of what he assumed was hand-knitted material under glass with a wooden frame. There was a quote he wasn't familiar with, skillfully embroidered into the material,

'Age doesn't always bring wisdom. Sometimes, age comes alone.'

On the armchair was unfinished knitting, and the smell of lemon-scented furniture polish was overwhelming. Near the television was a collection of movies. There were several box sets of Star Trek episodes, a documentary about the Vietnam War, a 'How to' guide: 'Electrical wiring for Beginners', 'The Sound of Music', and several DVDs about famous criminal trials.

Squeezed in between two of the DVD cases was a book, 'Clinical Paramedic Procedures'. On the coffee table was a magazine, open at a page advertising kitchen equipment. Three items had a large black tick next to them: an asparagus peeler, a hot-dog dicer, and The Egg Master. Next to the magazine was a small pot of 'Secrets of the Night' anti-ageing cream, and next to that, a can of what claimed to be 'face-slimming hair spray'. When Mrs. Mandrake finally came downstairs, she was wearing bright yellow plastic hair rollers and a red flowered dress, but she'd managed to miss most of her mouth with her pink lipstick. She looked like Ronald McDonald. He lowered his camera respectfully.

"Mrs. Mandrake?"

"Yes, dear."

"It's about your husband."

"He's not here."

"No, he's at the Police Department."

"I see."

"I would like to talk to you about your husband."

"Do you know him?"

"Not really."

"I see."

"Don't you want to know why he is at the Police Department?"

"He'll have a reason. He always has a reason for everything."

She sat in her armchair and started knitting. He cleared his throat. "Mrs. Mandrake! I am sorry to inform you, that your husband came into the Police Department this morning and made a statement. In this statement, he says that he is going to kill you today. We will charge him with making a statement of criminal intent, and hold him until his arraignment hearing on Friday. I will need to ask you some questions and take some photographs. I will also have to collect anything that looks suspicious and take it away for further investigation." Mrs. Mandrake continued knitting in silence.

"Did you hear what I said?" he asked.

"Illogical," she replied.

"Do you have any idea why your husband has done this?"

"I'm a Klingon, not a psychiatrist," she smiled and continued knitting.

Sergeant Wattana felt himself losing patience. "You don't live in space Mrs. Mandrake."

"No, I live in Spoons, I only work in space," she replied.

Sergeant Wattana placed his hand over her knitting to get her attention.

"Please, Mrs. Mandrake; you are not being cooperative."

From the corner of his eye, he noticed four deep indentations in the carpet to the left of Mrs. Mandrake's chair. It was clear the chair had recently been moved from its previous position to its present location in front of the window. She noticed his eyes move from one location to the other.

"Yes, my husband suggested I move the chair to catch the light from the window when I'm knitting. He can be considerate, for a -HU-MAN." She followed his eyes again, from the chair to the window and back to the chair. She realized what he was thinking. "You don't believe my husband has got somebody to kill me through the window?"

"I'm responsible for your safety Mrs. Mandrake. I would prefer if we moved the chair back to its original position and closed those curtains."

Mrs. Mandrake gave a heavy sigh as she watched him move the armchair to the left, exactly where it had been. He closed the curtains dramatically, as you do when you are a police officer. Mrs. Mandrake turned on the main light and a ceiling fan before sitting and resuming her knitting. She looked up at his face. He saw two large tears beginning to form in her eyes. "May I say, I have not enjoyed being with you HU-MANS? I find your foolish emotions a constant irritant. Of my husband, I can only say this: I will chase him around the moons of Nibia, around the Antares maelstrom, and round Perdition's flames before I give him up. I have been, and always shall be, his wife."

Sergeant Wattana recognized most of the quotes she had used from Star Trek movies. She resumed her knitting.

"SO-HVA-D –PAGH- VIJATLH-HU-MAN! I have nothing more to say to you, HU-MAN!"

He stepped back.

"Ok, she may be mad, but I still have a responsibility to protect her," he told himself. "She sure is a little strange, but is that any reason to kill her?"

The answer he gave himself after a pause was, "Of course not."

But he felt a little guilty that it took him that long to answer his own question.

Over the next hour, Sergeant Wattana took more photographs in the living room and every other room, collecting pills, potions, and objects, labelling small plastic bags and containers before carefully depositing the not-very-suspicious materials in sealed evidence bags.

He was in the driveway checking the car when Mrs. Mandrake emerged in a coat and carrying two shopping bags.

"What are you doing, Mrs. Mandrake?"

"It's 11 am, Wednesday. I always take the car into town and go shopping at 11 am on Wednesday."

"I'm sorry, but that is impossible this Wednesday. You can beam down tomorrow," he said sarcastically. "You will have to stay on the space station today," he insisted, trying to get into the spirit.

"But I always go shopping at this time." She protested.

"Yes, and that's why you shouldn't do what you normally do, especially today."

Mrs. Mandrake didn't argue. She turned around and went back inside the house but on the way, she whispered a few more Klingon curses under her breath.

After a few minutes, he followed her. She was in the living room, back in her armchair, wearing thick reading glasses and knitting rapidly. The curtains were still closed, and the ceiling fan was still circulating air around the room. She seemed content with her knitting. The blades of the fan whirred and purred like the wings of a giant moth and Mrs. Mandrake dreamed her favorite dream.

The dream of galaxies far away, a comfortable, predictable 'Star Trek' theme Park, where everybody spoke American English and reversing the polarity was the solution to every engineering problem. A place where robots had feelings and clones had the same haircuts. Where aliens had silly foreheads with invisible force fields to save on the budget. Evil alien planets where music, painting, and dancing were banned and there was always a place called the 'Forbidden Zone'.

Aliens had pulse weapons that fired slow-moving blue blobs of light and made friends with the teenage genius on Earth who had discovered an entirely new field of science in his bedroom. Alien women had extra breasts, still used lipstick, and could be bribed with a dress. Alien computer security could be cancelled by just saying, 'override'.

She loved this dream.

Sergeant Wattana had, by now, returned to the Mandrake's car outside and had started looking underneath at the wheels. Eventually, he was satisfied that the car had not been tampered with, at least as far as he could tell. He returned to the house, sat at the kitchen table, and started to read one of the books from the car's glove compartment, 'The Devil Made Me Do It'.

No more than a couple of hours passed. He went occasionally into the living room to check on Mrs. Mandrake. Everything seemed as it should be. Presently, he heard Mrs. Mandrake flushing the toilet. She was noisily clearing her throat. He heard another flush.

He waited.

…and waited.

"Are you all right?" He was concerned.

"Oh yes, dear! I just felt a little sick, that's all. It's probably all the stress of today."

She did look pale, he noticed. "Did you vomit?"

"No, I wanted to but couldn't. I am fine now honestly."

Sergeant Wattana decided that he was taking no chances. Anyway, he enjoyed any excuse to click on his radio. It popped and crackled. "I have a 10-38, Cobbler's Knob. Repeat, I have a 10-38 - Ambulance required, Cobbler's Knob."

Mrs. Mandrake looked alarmed. "Oh no, please. There is no need. I feel just fine now. A little nauseous, that's all."

Sergeant Wattana sat with her in the living room until the small Spoons paramedics' ambulance arrived. He told himself that one of the advantages of living in a small town was that, in an emergency, the ambulance could get anywhere quickly. Mrs. Mandrake was now looking old and vulnerable as he walked her out of the house toward the ambulance. She looked frail, not at all like the fearsome Klingon warrior that had greeted him.

"I'm never ill," she said, but then she continued, " but it's strange, my husband has been sick quite a lot recently."

"Sick?" Sergeant Wattana noted.

She looked back at the house.

"Yes, sick over the past three months. I think it's because he stays up at night, reading for hours. Sometimes I hear him being sick in the toilet. Maybe we're both coming down with the 'flu or something."

Bobby Bodean, the ambulance paramedic, was always surprised at how big everyone was in Spoons and Mrs. Mandrake was no exception.

"Was it only in America that you can be poor and fat at the same time?" He would ask himself.

Not wishing to offend his larger patients, he'd long ago stopped his practice of assisting them into the back of the ambulance and helping them to lie down on the gurney. He had found it difficult to disguise his bulging eyes, red face, and breathless choked groaning as he tried to take up the strain like an overloaded donkey. Instead, he politely pointed in the general direction like a Sunday afternoon traffic cop.

As Mrs. Mandrake cautiously climbed into the ambulance, Bobby Bodean nodded toward the gurney inside and asked her to lie down, making sure he gave no hint with his poker-faced expression that he was not going to assist her in achieving this challenging manoeuvre.

He then asked the Sergeant a few questions, especially if Mrs. Mandrake had vomited or not. He secured the doors behind him and unfolded a white sheet, spreading it over her body, "it made her look like Antarctica," he thought. He removed it. "I don't think we will need that after all."

"I know I'm a little overweight," she said softly.

"Just try and make yourself comfortable dear," he said, not wanting to dispute the definition of the word little.

"I do try to avoid anything that makes me look overweight," she added.

"Like mirrors and bathroom scales," he thought.

"There, there now, don't worry," he smiled.

"Is it genetics do you think?" She inquired.

"No, it's pizzas and cheesecake," he nearly said aloud. "You will be fine, there's nothing to worry about. We will give you a quick check-up. You'll be back home in an hour or two." He said routinely.

61

The ambulance started its engine and Sergeant Wattana, having secured the house, quickly followed in his Chevrolet. The paramedic hit the wall with his fist to tell the driver to move off. He followed the usual procedures, checking her breathing and circulation and her airways for blockages, Everything seemed fine. He inserted the nasal cannula, giving her oxygen at two litres per minute. She felt uncomfortable and asked him if oxygen was really necessary. He told her to relax; there was a procedure to follow. "Just to be on the safe side," he reassured her.

The I.V. drip he administered was known to the medical profession as 'Ringer's, a sterile solution of calcium, potassium chloride, sodium chloride, and sodium lactate in water to treat dehydration and replace electrolytes. He placed a cool cloth on her forehead. "This will help your nausea," he said quietly. He gave her the usual dose of 25 milligrams of Phenergan, through the I.V. along with some antihistamine. Her blood pressure, heart activity, pulse, and level of consciousness were all normal.

Then, unexpectedly, her heart stopped! There was no warning.

She didn't look as if she was in pain or distress of any kind. She just lay there as though asleep but she was sweating and her body had gone rigid. It looked like a cardiac arrest with no warning. The paramedic immediately screamed at the driver.

"Jesus! She's arrested! Put on the siren! Get us to the Medical Center fast!"

He couldn't understand it. He'd followed the procedures exactly. But now her pulse and her blood pressure readings were highly abnormal. Just a few seconds before, she'd been perfectly normal. He attempted to confirm cardiac rhythm with the Monitor. He started CPR. He'd never seen anything like this before.

"This couldn't be happening!" He mumbled anxiously.

"Her airways had been clear and secure. There were no blockages for the oxygen. He'd got I.V. access easily with no distress."

The ambulance swerved around a corner just as he was giving her the first dose of Epinephrine. He was thrown hard against the side of the ambulance. He looked at her rigid and still body.

"Damn!"

There was no response to the Epinephrine. Mrs. Mandrake's pulse was now erratic. "Some evidence of hypoxemia, oxygen levels in the blood were decreasing," he observed. He gave a second dose of Epinephrine.

He was just about to begin to defibrillate when her heart started again, but she had a fast heart rhythm. All he could do was continue with the I.V. and CPR, and the hyperventilation with 100% oxygen he told himself despairingly.

But it was all too late.

Mrs. Mandrake was dead by the time they arrived at the Medical Centre.

Mr. Mandrake lay on the jailhouse cell bed. By the time he turned his head and casually glanced at the clock through the cell bars, it was 2.03 pm.

He smiled.

Chapter Ten

Outside, on the sidewalk in front of her shop 'Shooz', which sold shoes, Dolores was correcting a mistake on a sign in the shop window. She was changing 'Buy One - Get One Free' to 'Buy One Pair - Get One Pair Free'. That's when she got the phone call.

"Mr. Mandrake, a teacher at the High School, has killed his wife and has been arrested," the anonymous caller informed her.

Dolores immediately phoned Mrs. Wilhelmina Dawkins, who was kneeling on the floor inside her shop - 'Carpets People Can Walk On'. She had just finished re-labelling all the $400 rugs to their new 'Bargain Sale' price of $499 when she got the phone call.

"Mad-duck arrested at high school for killing his wife!" she repeated, disbelievingly. "My God! Who the hell is Mad-duck?" Wilhelmina phoned Pastor Jack Lovetree who, after counting the week's profits in the Baptist Church, was getting ready to go to the bank when he got his phone call.

"Lord have mercy, Mrs. Dawkins! y'all sure? You say a man ducked into the high school after killing his wife and was arrested?"

Abner Bracegirdle was asleep in his office at the Spoons Savings and Loan Bank when Pastor Jack Lovetree burst in and dropped a bag of money on the manager's desk with a loud clanking thump.

"Abner, wake up! A man has been arrested for killing his wife and a duck in the High School."

Mr. Delaney, manager of the Crazy Horse Bar and Grill, overheard the conversation being first in line at the bank teller's counter, just outside Abner Bracegirdle's office.

After hastily depositing his money, he phoned Jed I. Knight who was busy in the Mini Mart, speedily removing the 'Sauna Masks' from the bathroom accessories shelf, following customers' complaints that their kids were wearing them around town to look like a serial killer.

"Missing Man-duck arrested for killing his wife who teaches at the High School?

Well, don't that beat all? Just shows y'un, best to always drink upstream from the herd," Jed remarked.

Mr. Cornfoot was carefully organizing his central display stand in the Boot Hill Gift shop, with a few extra items: a cowboy-boot birdhouse, some quick-draw beer-bottle openers, a gun-holster wine bottle holder, and a range of rubber-stick-on black Mexican moustaches, when he got the phone call from Jed I. Knight.

"Missing wife kills a duck at the High School? I dunno what y'all talkin' 'bout, but I'd better tell Arthur."

Mr. Arthur Macarthur and his wife, Magnolia, were baking their new line of pizzas with British fish 'n' chips toppings at the Mona Pizza when Arthur got the phone call.

"A Man disguised as a duck killed by his wife in the High School. Why was he disguised as a duck?" Arthur Macarthur inquired, reasonably.

Arthur Macarthur had no friends, so he called Mr. and Mrs. Chapawee, aka Chief Running Tab and Shopping Dear, who were inside the Little Big Horn Supermarket. She was spraying water over the out-of-date fruit and making sure that all the expensive items were at eye level. He was separating the bread, eggs, and milk into different parts of the supermarket so they weren't all together.

Mr. Chapawee got his phone call.

"Man disguised as wife arrested after killing a duck in High School."
He was silent for a second. "OK!" he accepted. Mrs. Chapawee
phoned the editor of 'The Spoons Bugle' and smartly negotiated free
advertising space for their Supermarket in exchange for the
exclusive front-page scoop.

On Main Street South the editor of 'The Spoons Bugle' couldn't
believe his luck.

A new headline for the weekly edition.

'MAN KILLS DUCK IN HIGH SCHOOL! WIFE ARRESTED!'

Chapter Eleven

"You have the right to remain silent. Anything that you say can and will be used against you in a court of law. You have the right to an attorney. If you cannot afford an attorney, one will be appointed for you free of charge. Do you have anything to say?"

"Thank you." Mr. Mandrake was a little disappointed. It looked much more dramatic on his, To-do list. He'd assumed the arrest would be more thrilling.

"You'll see the Judge on Friday morning." Sergeant Wattana locked the cell door.

Mr. Mandrake stretched his neck muscles. He looked out of the small thick window, high on the cell wall. Sergeant Wattana shook and rattled the door noisily to make sure it was secure.

"You murdered your wife!"

"Did I?" Mr. Mandrake sneered.

"You said you were going to kill her."

"True!"

"Now she's dead!"

"Also true!"

"You had a motive, the insurance money!"

"But, not the opportunity, Sergeant; you seem to forget that I have been your guest all day. You are my alibi."

"You're guilty; I feel it in my stomach."

"Fortunately for me, Sergeant, the law requires more than indigestion; it requires evidence."

"We'll get the evidence."

"You're just doing your job, I know."

"You know nothing about my job."

Mr. Mandrake smirked and through the small thick window glass watched the distorted image of a mallard duck flying in slow circles above the town.

"I know all about you and your job. Let me take a wild guess, Sergeant. You didn't join the South Dakota police force just to file traffic tickets all day. You assumed it would be far more exciting, like the movies. The movie where your angry boss, spitting out bits of doughnut, tells you to get in his office, right now, and shouts, 'That's it! You're off the case!' You've got 24 hours to solve the murder or hand in your badge!"

Mr. Mandrake laughed.

"You think you're clever." Sergeant Wattana barked.

Mr. Mandrake brought his expressionless face right up to the bars, close to Sergeant Wattana and whispered:

"For making a statement of criminal intent, I have been arrested and imprisoned. On Friday, I will plead guilty at my arraignment hearing to the charge of criminal intent. I will be found guilty and fined up to a maximum of two thousand dollars. I will walk out of court. Without evidence, you cannot proceed against me further. But, if you were right in assuming my wife's life insurance was my motive and right again in assuming my actions had a direct link to my wife's death, then you could charge me with the suspicion of committing the capital crime of murder.

However, the law requires more than an assumption; it requires a direct link, with real physical evidence. Did I have the motive, means, and opportunity to kill my wife? You have no evidence. You will find no evidence, and there is nothing you can do about it. You're too late, too slow, and too stupid…

…is that clever enough for you? Y'all have a nice day now."

Chapter Twelve

Tanapat and Heng sat together at the back of an unusually full afternoon English class. Nobody was skipping today! The two boys had told no one about Mr. Mandrake but rumors had started circulating early. The first clue that something out of the ordinary was happening came when teachers were seen huddling and chattering in corridors, a few mumbled phrases about ambulances, arrests, and who was next in line for Mandrake's car parking space. Every student sat at their desk in expectant silence.

"What's all this noise?"

Principal Nutter marched into class, carrying a pile of notebooks. He stood to attention, somberly, behind the teacher's desk, like Pastor Jack about to list his favourite sins in a sermon.

''I have a sad announcement'' he said, scanning every face in the room for an unrepressed giggle.

Tanapat and Heng looked at each other and down at their desks, because of an unrepressed giggle.

"Mr. Mandrake will not be back in school for a while. I'm afraid his wife passed away this afternoon. I am sure you are all as sad as I am to hear this news." Principal Nutter ran a disapproving finger over Mr. Mandrake's desk and looked at the resulting dust stain on his fingertip.

"Please get on with the homework Mr. Mandrake has set for you all.''

Principal Nutter gestured indifferently to a boy on the front row to give out all the notebooks and then sat heavily in Mr. Mandrake's teacher's chair behind the desk.

Everyone opened their notebook and eagerly read the homework assignment as though it might contain blood-splattered descriptions of death and destruction.

After a few seconds of reading, each student sighed with disappointment and, reaching into their bag took a paperback novel, flicked over pages, and pretended to read, as usual. Heng looked around the class at all the heads bent over books, some carrying the play-acting even further by pretending to make notes or, more probably, colouring in all the circles in the letters.

"Low key, Boss, look at them doing the most, busier than a shoeshine boy after a mud wrestling competition."

Tanapat tried unsuccessfully to mentally add English subtitles to Heng's latest comment. He looked over to Principal Nutter. He whispered through the side of his mouth at Heng. "I wish you wouldn't talk like that all the time."

"Everyone talks like that!" Heng lied.

Tanapat and Heng were the last to get their notebooks. They both looked at their homework assignment and then at each other, totally bewildered. They swapped notebooks and noticed that each of them had been given a different homework assignment. Tanapat was immediately suspicious.

"Heng, you need to go to the toilet."

"No, I don't." Heng protested as he sniffed at his trousers.

"Yes, you do!" Tanapat insisted. "On your way out, look at the homework everyone has been given."

Heng wasn't sure what was going on, but Tanapat's instructions were dramatic enough to raise him from his chair. He held up his hand. Principal Nutter looked across at Heng, coldly.

"What's all this noise?"

Heng twisted his face in overstated pain, "Sir, I need to go."

Principal Nutter wagged an indifferent finger toward the door.

Heng made his way through the grid of desks, furtively looking into as many notebooks as he could, on his way out of the classroom. Principal Nutter was opening all the drawers in Mr. Mandrake's desk and flicking through papers before finally picking his teeth with a sharpened pencil.

Most of the kids in class, now bored with the deception of reading the book, were passing notes to each other. The girls at the back were on their cellphones, hidden under their desks, and occasionally a boy at the front would laugh at the dirty joke one of the girls had just sent him in a text message.

Heng came back too quickly and Tanapat looked at Principal Nutter to see if he was going to make an issue of the unconvincing toilet scam. Principal Nutter was too busy looking through Mr. Mandrake's private letters and picking his teeth to notice anything.

"Mr. Mandrake is crazier than an albino in a snowstorm," Heng announced as the introduction to his survey results.

"What do you mean?"

Heng started to pretend to be reading his homework.

"They all have the same homework, but it's not the same as ours, they've got chapter four of 'Catcher in the Rye' and they have to summarize the main events.

Why do we have different homework than everyone else?"

Tanapat pointed at his notebook. "You think that's strange, look closer at my homework. It couldn't have been written by an English teacher. It's got mistakes. It doesn't even make sense!"

Both boys read Tanapat's homework task carefully. It was different from the rest of the class and different from Heng's homework task too.

Reading Comprehension Homework Assignment

Research the Declaration of Independence and the Constitution of the United States. Write some notes but be careful with spelling and grammar. Everyone makes A mistake; Benjamin Franklin was in a State about that.

I declare the British got very upset, about their tea. Its in the Constitution.

Further reading, 'The State of ILLINOIS versus Gates.'

When you have the information, bring your homework back to school to finish the task.'

Heng was alarmed. "Why is our homework different from their homework and why is my homework different from yours? What does it all mean, dude?

"I have no idea!" But Tanapat did have an idea. He remembered what Mr. Mandrake had said earlier in the morning to his dad,

'Well, Sergeant, the answer to that is beyond your comprehension. However, I think it is within your son and his friend's comprehension.'

Heng noticed something in Tanapat's homework.

73

"Look there Boss, two grammar mistakes, a missing apostrophe in 'its' and a capital 'S' in the word 'state'. Mr. Mandrake told us himself that only states that have the word state in the name get a capital letter, like the State of Texas, but the rest don't get a capital 'S' Mr. Mandrake would never make mistakes like that dude."

"Maybe he didn't write it." Tanapat hoped.

"Or maybe it's a clue" Heng whispered.

"A clue, what clue, a clue to what, Sherlock?"

As much as he tried, Tanapat couldn't escape a growing suspicion. Mr. Mandrake had murdered his wife and he had put clues to her murder in their homework, as unbelievable as that now sounded to Heng.

Heng laughed out loud. "MURDER! You're ten pounds of stupid in a two-pound bag, dude."

Principal Nutter growled, "What's all this noise?"

Tanapat and Heng manoeuvred their heads to eclipse the two heads at the desk in front. Tanapat whispered,

"Be careful with spelling and grammar, he's written here. Maybe he's telling us that the clues are the grammar or spelling mistakes."

Heng nodded his head. "That mule won't jump the fence."

As annoyed as he could be, whispering, Tanapat growled. "What the hell does that mean? Why can't you just speak English?"

Heng hid his mouth with one hand. "How could he kill his wife if he's down at the police department? It's impossible! Why would he leave clues? Why would he tell us? It's insane!"

Tanapat thought for a moment. "Don't you see? He's showing off! He wants to commit the perfect murder with the perfect alibi.

You can't have the perfect murder if no one knows about it. He said to my dad this morning he was bored."

Heng had a headache. "Yes, but if all he wanted to do was get himself arrested, he could have picked any minor crime. Why tell the police he was going to kill his wife and why tell us how he did it in our homework? Does he want to get caught?"

Tanapat grabbed Heng's notebook.

"He must be confident he won't get caught. He must think that even if we solve his damn clues there's nothing we can do about it. Nobody will take us seriously. Now let's see the homework he gave you."

'Your Reading Comprehension Homework:

I have marked your last essay.

no serious errors in grammar and spelling.

pAy attention to where words are in sentences.

Write about Marie curie, because I know you like science.

Read the first two chapters of her life from the internet.

I also recommend, 'history of Science: Marie Curie '.

Or 'ordeals of a Woman Scientist' also on the internet.'

Heng grinned, "This is easy! Look! The capital letters are all wrong. The second sentence should have a capital 'N', and the third sentence, a lowercase 'a. The fourth sentence, 'curie' is a name and should have a capital 'C'. Look in the sixth sentence, 'history of Science' should have a capital 'H', and the last sentence, the book title should have a capital 'O' for 'ordeals.' Put all the letters together and you get…."

Tanapat was ahead of him, "N-a-C-H-O. Nachos, I love Nachos, Mexican tortilla chips!"

Heng covered his mouth to speak again.

"I ain't havin' it! It can't be that simple."

"Why not, maybe the next clue is in a Mexican restaurant." Tanapat insisted.

Heng dismissed the suggestion. "Because he wrote. 'I know you like science...'"

"Yeah, so what, maybe it's Food Science!" Tanapat persisted.

"No! No! That's a reach dude. Mandrake is slicker than a hundred snakes in an oil barrel."

Tanapat rolled his eyes and sighed. "You just made that one up."

"Chemistry, it may be Chemistry! Those first two letters 'Na' could be Sodium, but it's no compound I have ever seen. There are no atomic weights, what does he mean, 'pay attention to where words are in sentences.' This is like so weird man!"

Heng started to drum his fingers on the desk.

"Talkin' clues like yooz da man,

like can't nobody do it like the Boss man can.

There ain't nuttin in the Vo-cab-u-lary,

its crazy talk, like im-agin-ary.

We ain't Mandrake's toys, coz …"

Principal Nutter slammed his hand on the desk.

"…WHAT'S ALL THIS NOISE?"

Chapter Thirteen

Sergeant Wattana knocked gently on Abner Bracegirdle's office door in the Spoons Savings and Loans Bank. Abner's voice boomed, "Ah, Sergeant! Come in, come in, what an expected pleasure. I've been waiting for you, boy. Come in." Sergeant Wattana opened the door apprehensively. "You were expecting me?"

Abner Bracegirdle, a colossal bald man, was holding papers and closing the drawer of a filing cabinet. He returned to his desk, and his substantial buttocks wriggled, squeezed, and squeaked their way back into his leather office chair like two trucks fighting over a parking space.

"Who would have guessed it? Mr. Mandrake, the old English teacher from the High School, just goes to show; you can pick your friends and you can pick your nose, but you can't wipe your friends on your saddle."Abner added incomprehensively whilst waving a pudgy hand generously toward the empty chair opposite.

Sergeant Wattana sat down and surveyed the clutter on Abner's desk.

"You know why I'm here?" he asked.

Abner looked at him as though Sergeant Wattana had said something particularly stupid. "Of course, I know why. You want to challenge Mr. Mandrake's life insurance claim, now that Mrs. Mandrake is tagged and bagged."

The Sergeant was surprised. "You know about that!"

Abner leafed through papers, licking a finger before turning each page.

"Mrs. Mandrake is now, as we say in the insurance business, a negative outcome. Of course, I know! The whole town knows! I have the insurance policy right here. You wanna know if we can stop his life insurance claim? Y'all wanna know if Mandrake is gonna be ridin' the gravy train on biscuit wheels."

"Where did you get that information?" The Sergeant quizzed.

"At the gettin' place, boy," Abner said dismissively. "Unless that is, you have some good news for me."

"What good news would that be?"

Abner spilt the papers onto the desk, leaned back in his chair which groaned and put his hands behind his head.

"Old Mandrake, close to retirement they say. Too poor to paint, too proud to whitewash, does his wife in for the insurance. Three and a half million dollars will make any husband who's gotta dead wife as happy as a pig in sunshine. Now you've come to tell me you've arrested him and we don't have to pay out. I got it all here ready for you. I suppose you can't blame the man for trying. Everyone wants easy money, boy. Put wishes in one bucket and bad luck in another, and see which one fills up first. Life ain't fair for damn sure; most people work like a dog, just to end up living like one. My daddy told me, that up to eighteen years old, a man needs good parents, from eighteen to thirty-five he needs good looks, from thirty-five to fifty-five he needs a good personality but from fifty-five on, he needs hard cash.

Now, you take this Mandrake fella, poor, but with brains; that's always dangerous."

Abner Bracegirdle unexpectedly leaned forward on his groaning chair and divided the clutter on his desk, like God parting the sea for Moses.

He pushed aside the paperweight- a blue liquid with two little floating penguins. He knocked over the cellphone holder – a rubber gorilla - and sent the pencil sharpener, shaped like a nose, rolling off the desk onto Sergeant Wattana's lap, at the same time bashing the two toy plastic eyes, which started blinking faster than a frog in a hailstorm. Finally, Abner carefully moved aside a small wooden sign which read, 'Give me coffee and I won't hurt you.' He carefully placed the Mandrake insurance papers in the reclaimed space of his desk.

"This is Mandrake's twenty-five-year-old Life Insurance Policy and they have never missed a payment. Death benefits totalling three million seven hundred thousand dollars and fifty-three cents, less the usual administrative costs, of course. We are preparing a check now for Mr. Mandrake in the sum of three million, five hundred thousand dollars."

The Sergeant was stunned. "The administrative costs are two hundred thousand dollars?"

Abner grinned, "They will be, boy, by the time we've finished. Of course, we'd rather not pay out anything at all, as you might appreciate. That's why I was hoping you had some good news."

Abner squinted at the pages.

"I have the relevant clauses right here. Where one spouse pre-deceases the other spouse, the surviving spouse, in this case, Mr. Mandrake, becomes the primary beneficiary under the policy agreement, so long as the said primary beneficiary meets the following conditions in the three-month contestability period."

Abner took a closer look at the last sentence.

"Only three months! You can tell it's an old policy. The contestability period is two years nowadays."

"What is a contestability period?"

Abner retrieved his spectacles from his jacket's top pocket, and wrapped the thin wire frames around his ears, meticulously balancing the lenses on his red nose.

"Under the provisions of the policy, there is a period, following the death of a spouse, where the insurer, that's us, may contest the life insurance policy under certain conditions. Let's see now. Ah yes, here we are, the material misrepresentation clause. Did Mrs. Mandrake have a pre-existing medical condition not disclosed to the insurance agent at the time?"

"I have no idea!" the Sergeant said vacantly.

Abner sighed, "Well, we'll skip that one for now."

"Next, we have the suicide clause," Abner announced mouthwateringly. "Did Mrs. Mandrake take her own life? Did she kill herself to settle debts?"

The Sergeant wasn't sure how to respond. "No, I don't think so."

Abner ignored him and continued to savour the words on the page.

"Then there's the dangerous activities clause, - I love this clause because it lists all those hobbies which were considered dangerous at the time the policy was written, in this case twenty-five years ago. Did Mrs. Mandrake engage in any of the following dangerous activities: auto racing, rock climbing, hang-gliding, or wood chopping?

"I doubt it!"

"Then how about volcano-boarding, limbo skating or crocodile bungee jumping? That Cobbler's Knob Hill cheese-rolling contest can be pretty dangerous, I have heard," he added helpfully.

"No!"

"What about Buzkashi?"

"What is Buzkashi?"

Abner read out the small print. "It's the national sport of Afghanistan. It involves galloping around a large area on horseback, with each of the participants trying to wrestle the carcass of a goat off the other.

"No!" Sergeant Wattana was certain about that one.

"No! Probably not." Abner agreed. "The aviation exclusion clause; was Mrs. Mandrake killed in a commercial plane crash or as a passenger in a private plane? The act of war exclusion clause: the insurer will not pay if the cause of death is a result of a war declared or undeclared."

Abner didn't wait for a negative response.

"That brings us to the homicide clause,"

Abner peered over the top of his glasses and winked at the Sergeant.

"This may be the meat on our bone. If the cause of death as listed on the death certificate is homicide? Is the primary beneficiary a suspect in a first-degree or capital murder, involving planning, premeditation, or malice? Now surely we can get a charge of second-degree murder, killing without planning, premeditation, or malice?

Tell me it ain't just a felony murder. Killing during the commission of another crime, where the murder isn't necessarily planned, and is the consequence of another offence. You're draining all the fun out of this for me boy."

Sergeant Wattana paused. "Maybe."

"Has he been charged?" Abner glared at the Sergeant optimistically.

"Well?"

Abner was disappointed, "So, I take it the answer is no."

Abner started to feel more positive as he read out more clauses from the small print in the policy. "The intentional or illegal acts exclusion clause. 'Did the death occur as a result of a physical assault causing grievous bodily harm, an aggravated assault with the use of a weapon and/or an excessive amount of force, robbery, burglary, kidnapping, domestic violence, harassment, or stalking?

Sergeant Wattana sighed. "None of the above."

Abner peered over his glasses again at Sergeant Wattana, "Has the primary beneficiary been arrested for causing or causing others to have caused or contributed to, any related action resulting in the death of the joint policyholder?"

"We don't know."

Abner was becoming impatient. "I'm afraid all that's left now are the two miscellaneous exclusion clauses. They may delay the payment of death benefits to the primary beneficiary. Was the deceased insane?" Abner skipped to the last item. "Is the primary beneficiary involved in an ongoing police investigation?"

"YES!" Sergeant Wattana exclaimed triumphantly. "GOOD!" Abner was relieved.

"...and no..." The Sergeant quietly added.

Abner threw the papers on the desk in exasperation. "What do you mean, boy? Don't just squat there with your spurs on."

Sergeant Wattana stammered out an insufficient explanation. "Mr. Mandrake has been charged with making a statement of criminal intent. He's in court on Friday morning, but he's pleaded guilty and there is no ongoing investigation. There is no evidence to link him directly to the death of his wife."

Abner stood too rapidly and took the chair with him. He pushed hard on the arms of the chair, struggling to release his butt from the chair's tight grip.

"Well, don't that beat all? Y'all as useful as a steering wheel on a mule. Is that all you got? You've got nothing. Now let me tell you a thing or two about a thing or two. If you can't link Mandrake to the death of his wife or charge him with something more than a piddlin' misdemeanour, he gets the lot! He gets a check for three million, four hundred thousand dollars."

"I thought you said it was going to be three million five hundred thousand?"

Chapter Fourteen

Mrs. Lin cracked Heng on the side of his head with chopsticks as he came through the front door. "Have you eaten? We have dump-ings!"

Heng moved his head but, as usual, he was too late. He could never get the timing right between taking his shoes off at the door and avoiding the chop of the chopsticks.

"Mom, don't do that!"

She pushed him towards the kitchen.

"Dinner soon! Go to fridge; drink Can-o-Cok."

She cracked him on the forehead with the chopsticks.

"Take off hat! Don't wear hat all time, you look like criminal."

Heng was embarrassed. Not only did his parents own a laundry, the most uncool, stereotypical job for Chinese people he could think of, but they also lived as though they were "fresh off the boat." This was why he never invited friends. He didn't want his friends to see all the little shampoo bottles in the bathroom, taken from hotels, or the hundreds of McDonald's ketchup packets in the fridge.

Nor was he ever allowed to sleep over at his friends' houses because his mom was always afraid that he would be "molested."

On his way through the living room to the kitchen, he greeted his father who was lying on the sofa watching television, enthusiastically clicking the remote control, still in its plastic wrap, searching for TV shows to be offended by.

What a blessing it was for his father, Heng had decided, His dad could now record TV programs and be offended later. Heng had always been a straight 'A' student, but to his mom and dad, 'A' stood for 'average' and 'B' meant 'Burger King' and 'C', of course, was for 'criminal'. In his parents' universe, Heng had three futures: doctor, lawyer, or accountant. Heng sat at the kitchen table with his can of Coke and pulled out his cell phone. His mom was poking a hole in the aluminium foil, which covered the gas stove rings.

"You phone girlfriend?" she asked. "Why you not date Chinese girl? You racist?"

Heng sighed.

Mrs. Lin opened and closed kitchen cupboards methodically pulling out jars, pans, and bottles. She organized her kitchen according to the Chinese tradition of "reuse, repair, and recycle". Heng was always amazed how his mom knew exactly where everything was, but she had explained many times that in Chinese culture, where things are, the location of something, has a special meaning.

The conveyor belt of food started early, drawing his father into the kitchen from the living room. Plate after bowl crowded the small dining table: shredded potatoes, steamed corn with soybean buns, stir-fried pepper, tomato and eggplant, chicken rack with cumin sauce, cabbage stew, and cold noodle soup. "It was good," Heng admitted. "But like all food in China, it's never just good, it's delicious."

His mother snapped. "Put phone away, you look like criminal."

Heng didn't want to eat; he wanted to solve the Mandrake case.

"You have two choice," his father insisted. "Eat now, eat later, have tomorrow."

"That's three choices." Heng accurately pointed out, as he prodded a fish head.

"You can waste food when you pay for food," his father added inevitably.

"Eat! Eat! Do you want die?" His mother prodded his belly with her finger. "You fat, why you so fat?"

She pushed at his plate. "Why you not eat? You think different if you not have enough to eat, crowded elevator smell different to small person."

"What is your homework?" His father politely enquired.

Heng rolled his eyes because the politeness was faked; it was a trap. His dad was going to give his 'education' lecture. "I have to do some research on the internet." Heng knowingly sprung his father's trap, to get it all over with as soon as possible. His father sucked noodles, loudly.

"Internet for perverts! Book is garden in pocket."

His mother ladled cabbage stew into a small bowl near Heng's elbow.

"Internet no good for learning," his father persisted. "Elephant tusks do not grow out of dog's mouth."

Heng struggled to work out the relevance of the remark. His mom dropped a knotted tangle of noodle salad onto his plate. "To get good job, you need good grades. Why you cannot be same as cousin Chung, he go Harvard?"

Of course, everyone with a Chinese name was Heng's cousin, according to Mrs. Lin.

"I don't have a cousin Chung," Heng pointlessly replied.

His father jabbed his chopstick at Heng. "If you did have a cousin he would go to Harvard. No good grades, you live in a cardboard box."

"...and criminal," his mother added.

Heng remembered that in his house, everything he did or said was inevitably going to lead to a life of crime or sudden death. If he didn't eat boiled herbs or chicken feet, or if he wore his socks in bed, he would die. Meeting girls, not doing homework, watching television, wearing a baseball cap, computers, music, burgers, motorbikes, having friends, and having friends with motorbikes meant that he was going to become a criminal. He had stopped listening to his mom and dad's babble and jabber long ago. He reminded himself of another Chinese proverb, 'Birds do not sing because they have an answer. They sing because they must.' It all became a dull droning background noise as he tried to remember his homework:

'Your reading comprehension homework:

I have marked your last essay.

no serious errors in grammar and spelling.

pAy attention to where words are in sentences.

Write about Marie curie, because I know you like science.

Read the first two chapters of her life from the internet.

I also recommend, 'history of Science: Marie Curie '.

Or 'ordeals of a Woman Scientist' also on the internet.'

"Mr. Mandrake knows I have an interest in science." Heng was now convinced that the clues in his homework were Chemistry clues.

If, as Heng suspected, the first two clues were capital 'N' and lowercase 'a', it would begin with the element Na - Sodium. He was reminded of what his mom had said often about where things are placed having meaning in Chinese culture. Maybe where these mistakes with the capital letters had been placed in the sentences had some meaning. Are the positions of all the mistakes in the sentences intended to give him the number, the atomic weight for each element, perhaps? Had Mr. Mandrake given him the elements to make a chemical compound?

Capital 'N' and a lowercase 'a' would be the element Sodium. But 'curie' should have a capital 'C', and the fourth word could be the number four. And the word 'history', the fourth word -another number four, should have a capital 'H'. The word 'ordeals', the second word–should have a capital 'O'."

Heng put the parts together in his mind, $Na\ C_4\ H_4\ O_2$.

What did it mean? He had no idea what it was. He did not recognize it from his Science classes at school. He needed to get to his room and do some more research.

Heng awoke from these meditations to a rare domestic silence. The kitchen table was empty, apart from the eye in the fish head staring accusingly at him from his plate. It was a silence that could only be explained by the hypnotic effects of television on his parents. This was his opportunity to escape. Suddenly, there was an ear-splitting scream from his mom.

"Your dad has pressed the wrong button again on the remote. What's PC mode, TV mode, DVD mode? Why do we need 500 channels, anyway? This is going to give your father a heart attack!"

Heng rushed to the rescue, tripping over the foot massager on his way. He had noticed long ago that his mother's English always improved when she was annoyed.

By the time he finally made it to his computer, it didn't take him long to find out what the mysterious chemical compound was and, more importantly, where the substance could be found. Indeed, what and where it was had been in front of his face all the time. Heng opened his wardrobe, where his many character costumes hung in their laundry plastic wrappings. He reached onto the top shelf, stretching and searching. When he had found the jar, he gave it a reassuring rattle to confirm the contents. He sat on his bed and unscrewed the top. Carefully and almost lovingly, he reached inside the jar and pulled out one of the large white pellets. He held it to the light, as though examining the facets of a precious gem.

"Na C_4 H_4 O_2 more properly known as Poly-Sodium-Benzdioxin, the bleaching tablets from the old paper mill. So that's why we had to go on Mr. Mandrake's boring school field trips to the paper mill."

Heng leisurely revolved the pellet between his thumb and finger. His mother's voice, on the other side of the door, broke the spell.

"I hope you not wear socks on bed. You will die!"

Chapter Fifteen

Tanapat wasn't hungry. His father was sitting at the kitchen table behind a newspaper. Pamela stood over a spitting frying pan containing four bulky burgers which were hopping and bouncing in hot fat. She was wearing a pair of bright red plastic 'Onion' Goggles - only $19.99 - with a foam seal and anti-fog lenses, energetically pressing up and down impatiently on the toggle switch of her new automatic onion slicer - only $29.99.

"It needs new batteries, Pamela." Tanapat pointed out wearily. "Why don't you use a knife?"

Pamela grabbed a spatula and flipped the burgers making the slabs of meat crackle and sizzle angrily. A voice came from behind the newspaper.

"Mrs. Mandrake said she felt sick, that's all. Sat in her armchair knitting, then felt sick and went to the bathroom."

Pamela massaged the burgers flat.

"A high school English teacher. It's shocking. Maybe they'll find something when they do an autopsy."

Tanapat's dad continued reading the newspaper.

"There's to be no autopsy. The doctor says there's no legal reason. Woman of her age, a heart attack, is statistically common, that's what he said. No suicide, no injury, no wounds, not a mark on her, no suspicious circumstances, just a heart attack."

Pamela spanked a particularly disobedient burger with the spatula and held up a large kitchen knife.

"Death was sudden, unexpected, isn't that suspicious?" he quoted.

Pamela chopped onions furiously. Tanapat's dad continued.

"In the case of a sudden or unexpected death, the law does not require an autopsy, unless the deceased person's family gives permission; that's what the doctor said. I don't think Mandrake will be giving his permission anytime soon."

Pamela lifted out three of the burgers and arranged them on Tanapat's plate, "I guess not."

Tanapat's father lowered the newspaper and glared jealously at the three-to-two burger ratio in his son's favour. He continued his news briefing.

"The doctor said autopsies are unpleasant to perform. The procedure is messy, it takes time, the selection of tissue samples, the review of specimen slides, the report writing, and there is money. The doctor said autopsies are part of his administration budget, with no payment until the end of the year. He receives the same small amount of money if he does autopsies once a day or once a year."

Tanapat knew that in church, it was bad manners to answer your cell phone, snore during the sermon or cut your toenails while praying. In his father's house, not eating the food was treated the same.

Likewise, not even attempting to climb the north face of Pamela's Burgers resulted in the same intimidating silence from her. Over three years, the kitchen had become a war zone.

"I'm not hungry Pamela; I'll go upstairs to my room."

"You have two choices," his father insisted. "You can take it, leave it or have it tomorrow for breakfast."

"That's three choices." Tanapat pointed out accurately as he prodded his plate with a fork.

His father pointed at Tanapat's plate. "What would you eat if I didn't pay for it all? What would you do if I weren't here?"

"Rent out your room," Tanapat replied sarcastically.

Pamela sniggered as she sprayed water over a plastic cactus on the window ledge, wiping the unconvincing yellow petals with a damp cloth. Tanapat watched as his father's mouth moved, but he had mentally muted it long ago.

"It was the same old rubbish. 'Money doesn't grow on trees,' and always ends with, 'because I said so!'"

Like every teenage boy, he had long known how to make his dad angry for his amusement.

The secret was to answer 'yes' to everything:

'Am I talking to a brick wall?' 'Yes!'

'Do you think I'm made of money?' 'Yes!'

'Were you born in a barn?' 'Yes!'

'Do you think your socks pick themselves up from the floor?' Yes!

'Do you think this is a hotel?' 'Yes!'

He had also learned to ignore his father's medical advice:

"' Don't eat that, you'll die!'

'Don't sit too close to the television or you'll go blind'

. 'Eat your carrots or you'll go blind'.

'Too much chocolate makes you blind'.

'Pull your face - it will stay in that position forever and, of course, you'll go blind'.

'Don't pick your nose; it'll make your nostrils bigger'.

'A little soap and water never hurt anybody', and, last but not least, the scary mutations parents develop when they have children,

"I've got eyes in the back of my head."

On top of that, he had to listen to his father's kindergarten mathematics lessons.

'I'm going to count to three and you'd better stop'

'How many times have I told you?'

'If you give 100 per cent, no one can ask for more.'

'Two wrongs don't make a right.'

Today, to save time, Tanapat was determined not to laugh out loud, when his father said, "When I was your age…"

His father finally pushed Tanapat's plate across the table toward him. Tanapat wanted to get upstairs to his bedroom and get to his computer, but the burgers, which Pamela had lovingly burnt, were stacked as high as a condominium and, surrounded with a regiment of French fries, looking like a castle under siege. His father folded his newspaper. Tanapat pushed his plate back toward his father, in the process knocking over the pepper pot.

He flung his chair back dramatically and ran out of the kitchen.

Pamela looked at the solitary plastic cactus and thought that maybe if there were two of them, it wouldn't look so lonely. She would go to the Minimart and buy another at the weekend, she resolved.

Tanapat found himself in the living room. He was angry. He looked at his father's briefcase on the coffee table and the camera next to it. He had the decision to make. The same decision all teenage sons have had to make from the beginning of recorded time.

Break something or steal something?

He opened the briefcase and saw some photographs. His dad had printed off copies from his camera, pictures of all the rooms in Mr. Mandrake's house.

He took out his cell phone, carefully placed the prints on the table, flipped them over one by one, and photographed each of them in turn. He tried to imagine that he was James Bond but without much success. 007 wasn't Asian, had lots of girlfriends, fast cars, loads of money, expensive clothes, and a life. Apart from that, they were the same.

He was still angry when he entered his bedroom and fell over the two piles of clothes on the floor, which he'd mentally labelled, "disgusting" and "disgusting but wearable", He sat by his computer, opened his emails, and, as usual, read the annoying message from Heng,

'Get a life!'

He typed back, 'OK, send me the link?'

He tried to think of new ways to upset his computer. He clicked the mouse repeatedly. A message appeared on the screen,

'The internet' cannot be stored in the recycle bin. Are you sure you want to delete the Internet from this computer?'

It always amused him. He clicked again;

'The Town of Spoons' cannot be stored in the recycle bin. Are you sure you want to delete the 'Town of Spoons from this computer?'

Smirking, he clicked 'Yes'. The computer's revenge was as swift as it was inevitable. 'Mouse not detected click OK'. Tanapat clicked furiously, 'User error; click OK to delete user'.

Pamela shouted. "What are you doing up there?"

"Playing!" he shouted back from muscle memory, rebooting the computer.

Pamela responded automatically and started to climb the stairs. "You'll have to ask your father."

Tanapat rolled his eyes; he would never get married. "After uninstalling Thai Wife Version 1.0, disable family, country, and children files before installing American update Pamela 1.1."

"If I get married," Tanapat thought to himself, "I'll try the demo version first, maybe even the trial version, but never the Home Edition."

He looked at the now rebooted computer screen. He hated his life!

"If only it was as easy as "Format: Life-Enter."

Pamela was now outside his bedroom door. She knocked quietly. "Are you sure you don't want anything to eat, dear?"

"PENNSYLVANIA!" Tanapat shouted.

"Do you want a drink with that?" she enquired.

He reached into his school bag and wrestled out his English notebook from his stinking sports gear, furiously flicking through the pages. Benjamin Franklin was from the State of Pennsylvania, that's why the word State had a capital 'S' next to the name Benjamin Franklin, he remembered.

He found the page and read his homework again. Taking a pen from the Superman cup on his desk, he started to scan sentences and underline words.

'Reading Comprehension Homework Assignment

Research the Declaration of Independence and the Constitution of the United States. Write some notes but be careful with spelling and grammar. Everyone makesA mistake; Benjamin Franklin was in a State about that.

I declare the British got very upset, about their tea. Its in the Constitution.

Further reading, 'The State of ILLINOIS versus Gates.'

When you have the information, bring your homework back to school to finish the task.'

He opened the search engine 'TypoBuddy', and frantically typed in 'Declaration of Independence, Pennsylvania.'

Pamela shrugged and went downstairs in search of something in the fridge called, 'Pennsylvania'.

He found a web page, which allowed a keyword search of the entire original Declaration of Independence document. He typed in 'Pennsylvania'. He punched the air in victory. "There it is - 'Pensylvania', with one 'n' missing, a spelling mistake in the original Declaration of Independence document. He was sure he had discovered a Mandrake clue, the letter 'n'. He read the next part of the homework task,

'Its in the Constitution.'

He read it again. "What is in the constitution? If Heng was here…," he thought. "He's much better at English than me. It's easy for Heng."

Tanapat went to a small mini fridge his father had reluctantly allowed him to have in his bedroom and pulled out a can of Coke. He emptied the Superman cup of its pens, pencils, and one metal spoon and poured it from the can. His eyes never left the homework. He saw something important and wondered how he had missed it. The capital 'A' in the middle of a sentence, 'Everyone makes A mistake…' Tanapat drank heavily from the cup of victory, spitting out bits of pencil fragments and dust left behind in the cup.

Now he had two parts to the puzzle, N-A.

He read the next sentence. 'I declare even the British got very upset, about their tea.'

He made a temple with his fingers, resting his chin on the tips and reading the sentence over and over again, pretending he was Sherlock Holmes just in case looking clever might make a difference. After five painfully long minutes, he had no idea! Then Tanapat heard Heng's voice downstairs in the kitchen.

"Yo, what's good, Mrs. Wattana? I've come to do homework with Tanapat if that's OK." Heng looked Pamela up and down, playfully.

"Wow! Mrs. Wattana, you make me feel some type o' way. You are prettier than melted butter on mashed potatoes."

Tanapat listened to Heng flattering Pamela and stared longingly at the baseball bat leaning upright in the corner of his room.

Pamela blushed as she melted like butter on mashed potato. "Do you think so Heng? I did my hair differently, I guess," she lied. Pamela, still blushing, closed the back door behind Heng. "Would you like something to eat, Heng? I'm making something for Tanapat." She walked past a mirror and checked her hair.

"That would be great, Mrs. Wattana. I'm so hungry I could eat the legs off a low-flying duck."

Tanapat shouted as loud as he could, hardly disguising his embarrassment.

"Get here Heng!" There was the sound of clumsy feet on the stairs, trot, clomp, stomp before Heng burst into the bedroom like a S.W.A.T. team without a warrant.

"What's happening, Bro?" Heng dropped and bounced on the bed.

Tanapat looked him over with contempt. "What the hell are you wearing?"

Heng had his hair in a kind of English public school side parting. He was wearing a light blue shirt and a brown bow tie, a tweed jacket with brown leather elbow patches, and tight black pants which ended a good inch above the ankle held up with red suspenders. He was also wearing tan-coloured lace-up shoes.

"You look like Doctor Who!" Tanapat rolled his eyes.

99

Heng sounded hurt. "Detective, init!"

Tanapat passed his notebook to Heng.

"Whatever. Look, I've found some clues in my homework, but I am stuck."

Tanapat explained and pointed hurriedly at what he'd discovered so far.

"It's easy, dude! Look, he's telling you all the clues are grammar or spelling mistakes. British tea won't be the tea you drink; it will be the letter 'T'. Declare would be the Declaration of Independence."

Tanapat felt stupid, "I knew that!"

Heng pushed Tanapat aside from the keyboard and typed the words, 'British- Declaration of Independence-'T'. Heng wriggled his arms out of his Hershel backpack like he was shedding skin, before holding out both his palms waiting for Tanapat to slap.

"See it? The Declaration of Independence, look here, 'Nor have we been wanting in attentions to our Brittish brethren.' British is spelt with one, 't', not two t's, a spelling mistake in the original Declaration of Independence, go figure."

Tanapat recited the letter clues so far, "N-A-T"

Heng glanced at the notebook but continued to type. Tanapat locked the bedroom door. "We need to look at the rest of my homework!"

"Way ahead of you, Bro" Heng replied.

They scanned the remainder of his homework together, but Heng had already started to type, click, and scroll. The rest of the message from Mr. Mandrake was confusing for Tanapat. Heng pressed the 'enter' key heavily.

"Mr. Mandrake is nuttier than a squirrel at a peanut festival."

Tanapat ignored him. "What is Mandrake trying to tell us?"

Heng pointed to the screen and smiled. "Boss, you're dumber than a coal bucket."

Tanapat placed both his hands on Heng's shoulders, temptingly near his throat, and whispered.

"Yes, and now I'm madder than a one-legged man at a barn dance. I swear - if you don't stop talking like that redneck Jim Bob, I'm gonna open a 'can of whup-yo - butt'.

Heng pointed at the computer screen showing the results of his search, whilst making a mental note of the phrase, 'can of whup-yo -butt' to use in conversation.

"Its in the Constitution…' should be, 'It's in the Constitution…' a contraction. He turned back to the computer excitedly. He typed 'Constitution of the United States -grammar errors - 'it's', into the search box. The reply was not long in coming

'In the original Constitution of the United States, written in 1787, there was, indeed, a mistake.' His eyes darted across the text on the screen.

' Article 1, Section 10, Clause 2. No State shall, without the consent of the Congress, lay any imposts or duties on imports or exports, except what may be necessary for executing it's inspection laws.'

"There it is! ' …'it's- inspection Laws…' it should be 'its' inspection Laws, with no apostrophe. Mandrake left out the apostrophe in the contraction to point us to the mistake in the Constitution."

Tanapat finally put all the letter clues together. "N -A-T-ITS"

Heng positioned the cup of Coke carefully on the desk ready for his revealing experiment.

"What is a Natits?" Tanapat watched as Heng moved and positioned the cup on the desk.

"The Homework clues are letters, N -A-T-ITS. But what do they mean?"

There was a long pause before both boys had finished mentally reordering the letters like in Scrabble. They glared at each other and shouted simultaneously,

"TITANS!

It's the name of the Spoons High School Basketball team!"

Tanapat was not happy, however. "But, what about the rest of it, further reading, 'The State of ILLINOIS versus Gates?"

Heng brushed his doubts aside. "We have to go to school to find the next clue and it's something to do with the Titans Basketball team."

He had to admit that Heng was probably right. "Maybe you are as smart as you think you are but there's more!"

Tanapat quickly connected his phone to the computer and started to display the photos of Mr. Mandrake's house one by one on the screen.

Heng immediately noticed there were two pictures of the living room, but they were different from each other, taken, presumably, at different times. One picture showed Mrs. Mandrake's armchair in front of the window, while the other had the chair moved to the left with the window curtains closed. He also noticed that not all the rooms in the house had been photographed. There were no pictures of the bathroom.

There was a sharp knock on the bedroom door. Both boys instinctively made to hide the notebook. That was what you did when the adults were near your bedroom –you concealed whatever you had been doing. There was no real need to hide anything; it was merely a teenager's second nature. From outside the door came Pamela's motherly voice.

"Tanapat, I have brought something to eat for you and Heng."

Before opening the door Tanapat pretended to tidy the room by kicking objects randomly in different directions. It was difficult for him to take in what he saw next. Pamela was carrying a tray, on which were packets of 'Pennsylvania Homemade Cookies'. She'd gone and found some food called Pennsylvania. Tanapat wondered if, three hundred years ago, his stepmother might not have been burned as a witch for that little trick.

Pamela looked past Tanapat and glanced at the picture on the computer screen. It was a picture of an armchair in the Mandrake house with some knitting resting on one of the chair's arms. Tanapat moved in front of the screen, attempting to block her view with his own body.

"My God!" she said startled.

Tanapat felt immediately guilty. "Now don't upset yourself, Pamela..."

She interrupted, "...the knitting in the picture. That's the intarsia knitting stitch. So hard, they say it is the hardest stitch to use in knitting. You need to concentrate when you knit with that stitch."

Between the incredible coincidence of food somewhere in the house called Pennsylvania and the irrelevant information about knitting, both boys fell into awed silence. Pamela waited until both boys had taken some cookies before she left the bedroom, still shaking her head in amazement that someone in Spoons knew how to knit with intarsia knitting stitch. The boys watched her as she floated across the room like a ghost and closed the door gently behind her. Heng was the first to move. He opened his backpack and reached into it. Tanapat sat on the seat in front of his computer with his cup of Coke.

"Well, what about your homework Heng?" Tanapat asked.

Heng's response was to remove from his backpack a large white pellet, looking rather like some kind of horse medicine from the Feed Store, and casually drop it into Tanapat's cup of Coke. The cup exploded in violent fizzing and bubbling, sending Tanapat spinning back to get away from the alarming spectacle.

The white pellet danced and sputtered around the surface of the Coke in faster and faster circles, hitting the sides of the cup, as though it were trying to escape, and giving off smoke. All this was accompanied by sounds of plinking, tinking and finally glooshing, as the pellet decreased in size and finally disappeared.

Having enjoyed the sight of the terrified Tanapat, Heng asked,

"Now, do you want the good news or the bad news?"

"What the hell was that?"

"That..." Heng proudly announced, "...was Poly-Sodium-Benzdioxin.

They used to use it in paper mills to bleach paper pulp white -- until it got banned. What you saw was the sodium in the compound reacting with the liquid in the cup.

"I don't get it!" Tanapat nervously looked down into the cup.

"My homework," Heng shoved his notebook in front of Tanapat's face.

'Your reading comprehension homework:

I have marked your last essay.

no serious errors in grammar and spelling.

pAy attention to where words are in sentences.

Write about Marie curie, because I know you like science.

Read the first two chapters of her life from the internet.

I also recommend, 'history of Science: Marie Curie '.

Or 'ordeals of a Woman Scientist' also on the internet.'

Heng reminded Tanapat. "Mandrake had left clues in my homework as well, remember? Capital letters where there should be none, and those lower case letters should be capitals, N-a-C-H-O"

"Yeah I remember, Nachos, Mexican tortilla chips, delicious!"

Heng's voice took on an admiring, almost respectful tone. "Mr. Mandrake has been clever. It wasn't only the mistakes in capital letters; it was where in the sentence the mistakes were. Tanapat bit hard into his Pennsylvania Cookie, nearly cracking a tooth.

"Still don't get it!"

Heng persisted with his Chemistry lesson.

It's not Mexican tortilla chips. It's $NaC_4H_4O_2$- Poly-Sodium-Benzdioxin. The mistakes were the letters, and the positions of the mistakes gave the atomic weights.

Tanapat spat out the remains of the cookie in disgust. "I still don't get it!" Then, finally, he did get it!

"He poisoned her!" he shouted. "That's great! I mean, poor Mrs. Mandrake. So, what's the bad news?"

Heng looked defeated. "It's like so like totally not poisonous, dude! Poly-sodium-benzdioxin is harmless to humans. You can inhale it as a gas, but it is like totally safe."

"Where did you get this stuff?" Tanapat looked inside Heng's bag.

"Same place Mr. Mandrake got it. Do you remember all those dumb school trips to the old paper mill? There are hundreds of those pellets in the old paper mill if you know where to look. This is the real reason he wanted to go there, I'm sure of it. Poly-Sodium-Benzdioxin was used for bleaching paper pulp white."

Tanapat shrugged, "It's a dead end! He's messing with our heads."

"Yep, looks that way!" Heng reluctantly agreed.

"There's another problem," he continued. "Even if it were poisonous, the effects from the gas released when Poly-Sodium-Benzdioxin is in liquid lasts for about one hour maximum and Mrs. Mandrake would have to be directly in contact with the gas to inhale any of it. How did he manage to organize this, if he was in the Police Department at the same time? How could he be in two places at once?"

106

Tanapat remembered something Heng had said earlier,

"Heng, you said this stuff had been banned. Why, if it's so harmless? My dad said Mrs. Mandrake felt sick and went to the bathroom. There must be a connection. There has to be a connection."

Heng had an idea. "Come to the toilet."

Tanapat asked wearily. "Now, why would I want to do something like that?"

Heng rummaged in his bag, took out another of the pellets, and grabbed Tanapat's arm. "Come on, I want to show you something."

The small toilet off the hall landing was not large enough for two people, so Tanapat stood in the doorway to listen for any disturbances from downstairs.

"You said Mrs. Mandrake was feeling sick?" Heng repeated.

"Right, my dad said she was in her armchair, knitting and she felt sick."

Heng continued, "What do people do when they think they are going to be sick?"

Tanapat shrugged, "Throw up?"

"Yes, but where?"

Tanapat worked out; since they were in the toilet, the answer may be relevant to this fact, "Uh, in the toilet?"

"Yes, they go to the bathroom and lean their heads over the toilet bowl, and they puke and then they flush."

Heng cautiously lifted the lid from the toilet cistern and handed it to Tanapat. Heng, meanwhile, had balanced the pellet on the float ball inside the toilet cistern. He pushed the handle to flush. The float ball angled upwards pulling the flush valve chain tight, in turn opening the flush valve at the bottom of the tank.

The pellet slid off the ball into the tank of water and the tank began to drain promptly into the toilet bowl. The reaction of the sodium in the pellet, when it came into contact with the water caused an agitated dance of frenzied twirling, twisting, and flashing; jets of hydrogen were released which propelled it powerfully against the sides of the tank wall, as though it were desperately trying to escape. The water had only half drained when the pellet fizzled, dissolved, and vanished.

"So, what does that prove?" Tanapat had his eyes firmly fixed on the top of the stairs.

Heng was disappointed. "The reaction is too quick. None of the gas is flushed into the bowl with the water."

Tanapat impatiently whispered. "Even if it did, you said it's not poisonous."

"Yes," Heng admitted

"So?"

Heng sighed heavily. "I was sure this is how he did it. We're missing something. I'll have to do more research."

Tanapat pushed the cistern lid back into Heng's arms. "Yeah, you do that!"

108

Chapter Sixteen

The hungry duck scrutinized Tanapat and Heng from its perch on the bleachers next to the school's sports area. The two boys had waited for the school to close that evening and were now approaching the back entrance. The duck blinked, lifted one leg, and back-fired off a feather flapper.

Heng stopped and looked at the bird.

"What's wrong?" Tanapat quizzed.

"I heard something...No...That's impossible." The duck looked away innocently.

Tanapat pushed open the door at the back of the school, which led directly into the empty gymnasium locker rooms.

"It's open!" Heng was surprised.

"Of course, it's open. This is Spoons, Nuthook County, South Dakota. No one locks the backdoor."

"I didn't know that."

"You need to get out more."

They both entered the dark and clammy school locker room. The starving mallard stretched its wings to their full majestic span and soared off onto the evening breeze.

With their eyes burning and nostrils protesting, Tanapat and Heng tried to hold their breath longer than an Olympic swimmer. From arsenic smoke, which was used by the ancient Chinese against their enemies, to the ancient Greeks who catapulted clay pots filled with the intestines of rabid dogs over city walls; the use of chemical warfare has had a long deadly, depressing history. It has to be a matter for debate, however, if there has ever been anything so appalling, so terrible, odious, and shocking, as the fragrance of a high school locker room. The skunky, moist, musty smell of leather, dirt, grass, dried blood, hard soap, cheap aftershave, festering socks, and sweaty wet towels was overpowering.

For Heng and Tanapat, the school locker room was also the preferred site for torturing the school nerds, the gladiatorial arena for the official school bullies, and their official victims. The domain of 'mucho macho', where everyone's IQ dropped by fifty per cent the moment they entered.

Tanapat and Heng shared bitter memories of torment in this place. It was, on the other hand, the acknowledged headquarters and the place of post-match grief for Spoon's High School Basketball team, the 'Titans'. This was made more obvious by the seven lockers, reserved especially for the team, five for the main players, and two for the regular substitutes. The lockers were painted in the same team colours, blue and yellow. It was clear to Heng the next clue would be in one of those lockers, but as yet they had no way of knowing which one.

Tanapat pointed confidently, "That one!"

Heng scanned each of the seven lockers, "Why that one?"

"It's the one with a combination padlock, the rest open with a key, which we ain't got."

Heng stated the obvious, "but we don't have the combination."

"Don't we?" Tanapat smirked. He took out his cell phone and retrieved the photo he had taken earlier of the text in his homework.

"The last part Mandrake wrote in my homework assignment, 'ILLINOIS versus Gates.' Tanapat rapidly pressed buttons to access the Internet. He entered the phrase, 'ILLINOIS versus Gates.' There was a pause as he squinted to read the small text.

"Well?" Heng asked impatiently.

Tanapat read from the screen.

"The state of ILLINOIS has charged William Gates with vandalism for erecting an upside-down American flag, the traditional military signal for distress, in his front garden, as a protest against the election of the President." Tanapat read it a second time. "I don't see any numbers."

Heng snatched the phone and read it for himself. Tanapat strained to look at the phone screen upside down in Heng's greedy grip and was about to snatch it back.

"Now let me see," Heng said, pretending to know what he was doing. "If we add the number of letters, divide by the number of words...."

"...101771," Tanapat declared.

"What?" Heng looked at Tanapat who was grinning.

"The combination is 101771," Tanapat repeated without ceremony.

"How do you know?"

Tanapat grabbed the cell phone, turned it upside down, and placed it back in Heng's hand.

"Not the American flag upside down, the name ILLINOIS upside down."

Heng read the upside-down text, the inverted letters in, 'ILLINOIS', did have six letters which resembled the numbers '101771'.

Heng was disappointed. "It was easy!"

Tanapat reassured him. "We're kids, Heng, Mandrake knows that. He wants us to open the locker."

Tanapat approached and checked; the locker was indeed locked. He confidently rotated the combination dial on the small padlock, to the number, '101771' and the steel shackle clanked open. Tanapat cautiously opened the door. In the otherwise empty locker were two white envelopes. On one of them the name 'Mr. Wattana' was neatly typed, on the other 'Mr. Lin'.

He casually handed Heng the envelope meant for him. Heng looked at the envelope and his friend. Tanapat nodded his encouragement. The envelope wasn't sealed and Heng opened it and pulled out a piece of white paper with the name, 'Jerome Kern's typed on it. Heng turned the paper over to check if there was anything else. There was nothing more on the paper.

"Do you know anyone called Jerome Kern's?" He handed Tanapat the paper.

Tanapat also rotated the paper a few times. "Never heard of him!"

Heng, who was still holding Tanapat's cell phone, quickly researched the name.

He read aloud the Wikipedia reference.

"Jerome Kern, 1885 to1945, an American composer of popular music, blah, blah, blah. A native New Yorker, Kern created dozens of Broadway and Hollywood musicals in a career lasting for more than four decades, blah, blah, blah. He wrote more than 700 songs, including such classics as "A Fine Romance", "Smoke Gets in Your Eyes," "Can't Help Lovin' Dat Man," and, "Ol' Man River", blah, blah, blah…"

Tanapat interrupted, "…the name of the last song!"

Heng repeated, "Ol' Man River".

Tanapat laughed, "Old Man Rivers! That's it! You need to go and talk to old Mr. Rivers. That's the clue." Heng looked unconvinced. "Something's not right. This is too easy. Why Jerome Kern's, and why the apostrophe and 's'?"

Tanapat shrugged, "Jerome Kern's song, 'Ol' Man River', is the song belonging to Jerome Kern."

Heng was distrustful. "Yes, but he didn't need the apostrophe and the, 's'. All he needed to write was the name Jerome Kern and we would have found the song title anyway. We're missing something."

Tanapat, eager to discover his clue, did not share Heng's unease and ripped wildly at his envelope. He pulled out what looked like a large ticket but was horrified when he saw the name at the bottom.

"Oh no, it's the Mad General!"

Tanapat sat on the wooden bench in front of the lockers. Heng pulled gently at the ticket and released it from Tanapat's grip. He read the words aloud.

113

"Congratulations! This complimentary ticket permits you one free twenty-minute ride on my helicopter. To claim your free ride, please bring this ticket to the airport at the edge of town. The management reserves the right to decline customers who exceed the specified weight limit. There is a $50 surcharge for passengers who weigh more than 275 pounds.

-signed, *The General.*'

Heng's friend Tanapat, with his head bowed, looked "sadder than a bald man in a shampoo factory".

Tanapat sighed, "I have to go and see the mad general." Heng was in full sympathy. "Yes, he's certainly missing a few dots on the dice, his dogs are certainly off the leash, the elevator goes up, but the doors don't open, not all his soldiers are marching in line, he's lost contact with the mother ship. The hard drive is spinning, but the operating system needs installing..."

Tanapat snapped! "YES! I'VE GOT THE POINT!"

Heng sat next to his friend in silence, gave the ticket back, and started to fold his piece of paper, bending over each corner in half to make a sharp crease. Eventually, the transformation to a paper jet was complete and Heng launched it high and proud. Both boys gawked and swayed their heads as it soared, circled, and returned to Heng.

Tanapat abruptly reached out a hand and snatched it in mid-air. He carefully unfolded the paper and held it.

"Jerome Kern's paper", he exclaimed, "the paper belonging to Jerome Kern, not the song belonging to... The clues are Mr. Rivers and the paper. Mr. Rivers must know something about the paper mill." Both gave a triumphant high five.

Tanapat had recovered. "You go and see Mr. Rivers and I will go and see the Mad General." Heng partially covered his mouth and pretended to be a radio.

"Good evening Mr. Wattana and Mr. Lin. Your mission, if you decide to accept it, is to follow the clues and discover how Mandrake killed his trouble and strife. As always, if you or any of your team is caught or killed, the Secretary will disavow any knowledge of your actions. This tape will self-destruct in thirty seconds."

Chapter Seventeen

Heng had hardly time to change into more appropriate clothing when he was off on his mission to find Mr. River's house. According to Mr. Cornfoot, the Curator of the Nugget Trading Post Museum, the house was just outside town, two hoots and a holler away. Thinking he was now lost, Heng had immediately regretted asking Mr. Cornfoot for directions.

After a lot of instinctive guesswork and feverish consultations with his newly downloaded compass app, he had eventually found the dirt track leading to the old man's house, through the densely scented spruce, birch, and pine forest, about a mile outside town, near the old paper mill.

He paused and looked around.

"It was the kind of forest that was a favourite of bad horror movies," he thought, squinting through the evening gloom to see any evidence of an old wooden shack or cabin through the jungle.

"The kind of movie," he remembered, "where the victims always split up to get murdered separately and the stupid characters are as numerous as fleas on a farm dog.

Where the weird local tells you to 'turn left past yonder', where there's a shortcut through Demon's Creek onto the lonely road, the car never starts, and there's no cell phone signal, all bicycles have bells and dogs always know to bark at the bad man.

Finally, you reach the house in a storm, where the door knobs suddenly stop working, people run upstairs from the monster instead of out the front door, and the killer talks too much but only kids can see the floating furniture and talk to dead people."

Heng continued cautiously down the track now bathed in evening twilight shade. The tree-lined drive, with its low bending tangled branches, locked together in a life and death embrace, had cast their dark green lattice shadow on the gravel path before him. Wet and dying leaves trembled on the branches. Heng walked over the thick mat of green moss and grey gravel that seemed to swallow every noise his steps made. Sometimes, a broken rose, trapped and strangled in wild grass and shrubs at the side of the path hinted at happier times. He turned a corner.

"You have to be kidding me!"

Heng was taken completely by surprise! Where was the old west pioneer's log cabin, the gold prospector's shack, the wooden shed belching out smoke from the illegal liquor still? Where was the old man himself, dressed in faded work overalls with a ten-gallon hat, a pipe between his missing teeth, a pick-axe in one hand, and a hunting rifle in the other, falling drunk off an old mule called Luke?

Through the bars of a broken rusted iron gate was a grand mansion, an ivy-strangled chocolate box with two floors, evenly-spaced wooden shuttered windows, Greek-style columns, a covered porch with the remains of a mangled seat swing, a central double doorway and second-floor balconies stretching all around the house. In front of the leaf-covered steps, leading to the porch, was the famous sit-down lawn mower, waiting like an obedient pet for its master.

"Surely the old drunk doesn't live here?" Heng was baffled.

The gluttonous green ivy covering the great house had long ago stopped being decorative and was consuming the brickwork. The closed-shuttered windows concealed spacious but empty rooms with dank, foul air and forlorn shadows on floor and walls, ghostly images from the grand furniture that had once ornamented the interior, long since sold off to pay debts. The pine wooden balconies were rotten, the porch decomposed and the steps to the house a perilous, step-by-step lottery for none but the bravest.

117

As Heng reached the front entrance, someone within started to hammer on an out-of-tune piano, clinking and plinking an unknown tune. Occasionally, a dog howled like a demon and a man's voice barked, "Down Lincoln!"

A bird screeched and the voice would shout, "Shut up, Adolf!"

Heng pushed gently at the double front doors. There was a satisfying and predictable creaking as the doors sluggishly opened, pushed against something, and stopped. Heng squeezed through the small gap. The door had been blocked from opening by half a tree trunk. The tree had been hacked by an axe that was still deeply embedded.

Behind the door, the once elegant reception of the grand house was a junkyard. The blue and white floor tiles were scratched and broken. The walls were covered in blackened fungus-coated peeling wallpaper. The staircase to the upper floors was blocked with empty plastic bottles, copper piping, sacks of corn flour, yeast, and sugar, the main ingredients of one of the old man's famous brews, 'River Lightning, 'the devil's mouthwash,' 130% proof moonshine whiskey.

Heng walked over the scattered debris toward the sound of the piano. As he moved closer, there was the overwhelming rancid smell of half-chewed butcher's bones, bird droppings, stale whisky, cigar smoke, ancient paper, dust, and the leathery, caramel odour of old books. Heng's thoughts tumbled together, like his dad's underpants in the spin dryer.

What was on the other side of the closed doors that now lay ahead? He mentally wrote notes for a possible future horror script. He had to admit that he was a little scared. "What would my father say? 'Don't fry bacon when you're naked,' or something equally useless.

"I really must stop listening to him." Heng resolved again. Heng tapped on the stained door. A dog growled and the piano stopped.

Silence.

The old man rose from the piano stool and stretched out one leg like a dog having a pee. He turned to face the door. Heng reached for the doorknob, his hand slipping and sliding on a mysterious greasy substance until he was forced to use both hands.

The door opened.

The dog glared at Heng with one lip curled into a snarl. Heng frantically rubbed his hands to displace the grease on his fingers, as a parrot's head bobbing from left to right, as though it couldn't quite decide which eye to use for its disapproving stare. The old man looked at the apparition in front of him in the doorway.

"What the hell are you wearing boy?" he laughed.

Heng was offended. He was quite proud of his jungle exploration gear. An Australian Bushman's hat, speckled khaki-green camouflage jacket, dark green shorts three sizes too big, and mud-encrusted LeBron baseball trainers. He'd stitched on the deep green pockets himself, he recalled.

The dog closed both eyes and went back to sleep. Heng looked at the dog. The old man looked at Heng looking at the dog.

"That's Lincoln, my huntin' dawg. Never any use as a hunting dog," he added, "too scared of guns. Old Lincoln don't like guns going off behind his head."

Heng thought that sounded oddly familiar and somehow reasonable, although he couldn't quite remember why. "A great old dog," the old man mumbled fondly, "half Labrador, half Doberman. He'll bite your leg off, then bring it back to you."

The white-haired, unshaven old man, wearing a green silk dressing gown over a white shirt, red bow tie, no trousers, and brown army boots erupted into laughter ending in a deep, throaty smoker's rasping cough. The parrot finally decided on the left eye with which to view Heng with total disgust.

Heng walked forward a little, still trying to de-grease his hands. He was in a large library. Every inch of the walls was lined with bookshelves. Behind the old man was the upright piano and in the far corner of the room a single bed, a sagging mattress with an old blanket all surrounded with empty plastic bottles. He looked at the high ceiling and a shattered chandelier hanging like the skeleton of a long-dead prehistoric creature.

Directly above his head was a series of large holes in the ceiling plaster. He raised an eyebrow as he speculated about the insect that could have inflicted such damage. He scanned the titles of the books on the shelf nearest to him, 'Moby Dick', 'Carrots Have Feelings Too', 'Dr. Jekyll and Mr. Hyde', 'Fun with String: Volume 2', 'Dracula', 'To Kill a Mockingbird' and 'Pipe Insulation for Beginners'. On the rest of the shelves, was a gloom of tightly packed volumes, like tombstones in the half-light with different hues, and tinges of grey.

"My dad loves books. They make his heart beat faster," Heng recalled. "They're his paper dreams, his time machines, the keeper of secrets," his father would often say, pompously.

"What d'yer want boy?" Mr. Rivers sat back on the piano stool and crossed his legs.

"I'm doing a school project on the old paper mill," Heng claimed unconvincingly. "I've been told you worked at the old mill back when. Can I ask you some questions?"

Mr. Rivers swivelled around on the stool, positioned both hands over the piano, and threatened to drop them like two hammers on the tired old keys. He started to plinkety-plonk an old waltz. Lincoln the dog groaned.

"My family owned the mill, boy!" The parrot changed over to the right eye to glower at Heng. Mr. Rivers continued. "What do you wanna know?"

"Well…" Heng looked back at the parrot and pulled his tongue out at it.

"Why did the paper mill close?"

Mr. Rivers' animated hands and fingers plinked and plunked an accompaniment on the piano.

"No mystery boy! Spent too much, made too little. The family banker always said the easiest way to make a small fortune was to start with a big one. He was right! The rising costs for heating in winter, air-conditioning in summer, gas, water, electricity, higher wages, and lower profits, to hell with it! The bank owns this house now. They let me live here, in one room 'til they sell it off. Mr.

Rivers carried on playing and introduced his parrot. "That's Adolf!" the old man said appreciatively. Adolf the Parrot maintained one focused critical eye on Heng and blinked. The bird was every shade of green Heng knew of, with an orange half-moon beak. It had one foot on its food bowl, and the other foot busy as a toothpick.

"Do parrots have teeth to pick?" he wondered to himself.

Adolf started to pick pieces of fruit from his bowl, dropping them on Lincoln's head. From under Heng's feet began a deep distant rumble and throbbing below the floor. The chandelier swayed and jingled, and rugs lurched. Lincoln raised one eye. Powdery dust fell like snow from books and shelves, then a hissing, fizzing, burbling, gurgling, glug, and sputter. The sound of metal grinding and groaning, bending and straining, a sudden clang, like metal pans crashing to the floor.

The parrot squawked, "FIRE IN THE HOLE!"

A deafening *BAROOM* shook the entire house; the explosion knocked Heng backwards, stumbling and holding fast to the back of a chair.

Mr. Rivers stopped plinking. "Excellent! It's ready!" He turned to the dog. "It's gonna be a smooth one, this time, Lincoln, I can feel it"

The dog ignored him and sniffed at a piece of fruit, a near miss from the parrot bombardment.

"You see boy, my daddy was a bootlegger. That's where the family made its money to build that paper mill." The old man walked over to his bed and picked one of the empty plastic bottles, deciding to change it to a bigger empty plastic bottle.

"Back then you made real money haulin' 'shine over the State line. My daddy taught me and his daddy taught him. No rotgut, but clean and smooth, real quality. It'll put you down, knock you out, turn your lights off if y'un knows what I mean. There ain't any molasses or birch bark in mine. Good clean copper still, that's the trick, but you have to drink it quickly. Not like that old French wine where y'all bury the bottle for 40 years. Best moonshine needs to be drunk right outta the still."

He paced toward Heng, who was still waiting for the house to fall.

"You wait here, boy! While I'm gone, don't talk to Adolf. Do you hear me, boy? Whatever you do, DO NOT talk to the parrot. You hearin' me?" Heng nodded.

Mr. Rivers marched out of the room, eager to fill his bottle, his green silk dressing gown flapping behind him. Heng released his grip on the chair. He straightened his army jacket and brushed off ceiling dust from his hair.

He was beginning to think the visit was a waste of time. He listened for the return of Mr. Rivers. He walked around the room. He pulled a couple of dusty books from the bookcase and looked into the space left behind on the shelf. He tried to imagine what this library once had been when house servants polished its furniture, preened its books, and fluffed its cushions.

He was still determined to find a clue in the Mandrake case.

There had to be something. Why would Mr. Mandrake tell him to meet the old man if it wasn't important? The old man knew something; he must know something, but what? Heng paced up and down. The parrot also paced from left to right. The dog yawned. Heng circled the bird. Adolf the parrot fixed one large eye on Heng.

"Hello, Adolf! Who's a pretty boy? My name is Heng. Say, Heng! Hello, Heng."

He circled the bird in the opposite direction. It bobbed its head and fixed Heng with the other eye. "Hello, Heng, say hello, Heng. Can't you talk? Stupid parrot! Come on! Say something you brainless bird." The parrot turned his head to the right and considered the dog below, inviting Heng to follow the movement with his own eyes.

It squawked!

"LINCOLN...KILL!"

The dog, as though rocket-powered, launched itself through the air at Heng. Its ears flat, eyeballs rolled back in blood-lust madness.

Heng had managed to grip the snarling, hellhound by its throat, its contorted mouth and teeth in a fixed terrifying grin. Its hind legs dangling pathetically in the air, their power spent after launch and the dog's hot meaty breath on his face, a bony skull of fur and fangs, jaws gnashing, thrashing, snapping together, the devil's scissors.

There was a boom ...PKOW... a gunshot!

The dog immediately ceased its attack, howled, and dropped to the floor, like a rag doll, whimpering off to a corner of the room.

Mr. Rivers calmly lowered the weapon. A thin shower of white dust cascaded onto his head from the latest hole in the group of holes in the ceiling. "You talked to the parrot didn't you, boy?"

Mr. Rivers placed the handgun back on the table and started to pour the clean clear liquid from a plastic bottle into two short drinking glasses. "Get this down your neck." Heng, still recovering from the attack, grabbed the glass and gulped it all in one.

Mr. Rivers nodded wisely but sadly, knowing it may not have been clever for the boy to drink the brew so fast, the first time.

He sipped at his own glass and returned to the piano.

Heng couldn't quite remember the actual moment someone had emptied a nuclear reactor down his throat. But he was now sure about three things: he'd gone blind, he saw the parrot's beak curling into a smile before he went blind and his throat was melting.

Mr. Rivers placed his moonshine on top of the piano and started to plonk.

Heng was deep in thought. He planned to sit. Unfortunately, this plan required him to move, which was now impossible.

"I suppose we could have kept the paper mill open longer if it wasn't for the Penticott case." Mr. Rivers banged one hand heavily on the piano keys, producing a discordant chord. He stretched his little finger as far as it could reach and hit a higher key gently resolving the harmony.

"The Penticott case made us borrow a lot of money from the bank. That was the end."

Feeling sure he was near death, Heng managed to make a noise.

"What was 'The Penticott Case'?"

The old man stopped playing and took another sip.

"Abraham and Lewis Penticott worked at a paper mill in North Dakota, bigger than our mill, better than our mill, to be honest. The manager there used to give his workers milk to drink at the end of their shift, especially those who worked in the Bleaching Room. Bleach, the stuff that makes paper pulp white, came in large white pellets, good bleach it was, but it did stink and it made the air dry.

The men used to take the milk home and give it to their kids, men prefer something stronger than milk to drink at the end of a long shift. Anyway, one day those Penticott boys worked two shifts and, this time, they did drink the milk. They died within an hour. Both of 'em! Brothers, they were, quite sad! Just died, they did, on the floor of the factory. It was the bleach, you see. I mean the bleach itself is not harmful, but it reacted with the milk. Poisoned them both! Even a small amount can do it, those no-account, pencil-pushing experts said!

The management had to pay the Penticott family a truckload of compensation, and the bleach pellets were banned. Mill owners had to buy the safer, more expensive bleach. Yep! That was the final straw for us. What with the rising costs for heating water, electricity, higher wages, and, on top of that we had to buy the new damn bleach. They found out later if you drank the milk after you left the factory it was OK, nothing happened.

But if you drank milk within an hour of being exposed to the bleach gas…well……you're dead!

"SO THAT'S HOW HE DID IT!" Heng bellowed. He shook his head, back and forth violently, to clear his mind from the alcohol fog.

"IT'S A REACTANT!" he realized.

The old man stretched and cracked his fingers ready to torment the piano again.

"What boy?"

Heng spoke to the parrot, "…a reactant with the milk or probably an ingredient in milk!" The parrot turned its head away. The old man gulped the rest of his whiskey and the dog yawned.

"What you talkin' about boy? Forgot to pay the brain bill?"

Heng couldn't be happier. "He killed her! He killed her! $NaC_4H_4O_2$- Poly-Sodium-Benzdioxin, the paper-bleaching tablet, the gas isn't poisonous, until it reacts with milk or an ingredient in milk, within the first hour. That's how he did it!"

"I already told y'un this!" The old man appealed to the dog. "That boy couldn't find his butt with a mirror on a stick, Lincoln." The dog agreed.

Chapter Eighteen

The general's battered trailer at the edge of town was draped in a green and brown camouflage net propped up on four extended aluminium poles. The general himself clumsily tripped down from the trailer's two steps wearing a bright orange pilot's helmet and a leather A-2 flying jacket covering his mechanic's overalls.

To Tanapat, the ancient jacket made him look like an old leather wallet. The sleeves and back were decorated with graffiti. Large, gold, faded letters proclaimed 'Condor 464 squadron' and the image of a large bird with outstretched wings. On the sleeves and front were written anti-war slogans, 'Hell no, we won't go'. 'Drop the president, not bombs' and Tanapat's particular favourite, 'If war is the answer, it must be a dumb question.'

"Oh yeah, you must be Mandrake's boy. He said you'd come. Damn sure about that, he was. Didn't tell me you were a Chi-com? The general noticed Tanapat's bewilderment.

"Chi-com." he repeated, "Chinese Communist - 'Chi-Com', don't y'all do any history in that damn school?"

Tanapat could have confirmed he had not yet been treated to the History teacher's PowerPoint concerning the Vietnam War but settled, instead, for saying,

"I'm from Thailand."

The general adjusted his helmet. "Oh, you're a dink! What yo want, kid? I just got out my rack and I ain't had no C-rations."

Tanapat had cause to regret that of all the towns in the United States, he'd ended up in the one where no one spoke English.

Tanapat held out his complimentary ticket. The general ignored it. He knew why he was there and grunted.

"They say you were a pilot in the Vietnam War?" Tanapat enquired politely, trying to walk behind the general in step. The general paraded over to the helicopter opened the door, pulled out two pairs of gloves, and threw a pair at Tanapat.

"I wasn't no jet jockey if that's what y'un mean. I wanted to be in the Eagle flights or one of them C-54s, the Flying Crane, or a red bird, that is a Cobra helicopter. I got a slick in a Huey UH-1. In 'Nam, I had hardly finished basics when they sent us to the A.O. That's the Area of Operations to you. I was in Condor 'tween Thi-Tinh and Saigon rivers, Charlie was all over Cu Chi district. I was a shake 'n' bake pilot - got my sergeant stripes after two months. I was an early-out, because of an accident, then back on the Freedom Bird - Stateside."

Tanapat had no idea what he was talking about, or even why he needed gloves.

"They say you built this helicopter yourself?"

"That I did, boy. 30,000 dollars. A two-seater Delta," the general said proudly.

"Well don't stand there put them gloves on, the tourists love that kinda- thing. You can be my A-gunner on this boondoggle."

Tanapat climbed fearfully into the cramped passenger seat behind the pilot chair, not caring or wanting to know what a 'boondoggle' was, and the general leisurely spread himself out in front. He threw a clipboard back over his shoulder onto Tanapat's lap. "Read the checklist, make it loud boy! The tourists like that kinda - thing."

Tanapat obediently shouted out from the list. "Auxiliary fuel pumps off. Flight controls are free and correct. Instruments and radios checked and set, Altimeter, Directional gyro, Fuel gauges…"

Tanapat was alarmed to hear a loud grinding, growling, and sputtering as the engine started. Then a whining and whistling from the turbine, faster and faster and faster until the whoosh and 'whup-whup-whup' of the rotor blades merged into one pulsating drumbeat, like a badly maintained washing machine. Tanapat shouted out from the checklist.

"Magnetos, engine idle, flaps as required, parking brake off…"

"…Hold on to your butt, boy." The general opened the throttle, at the same time as his feet hit the foot pedals controlling the tail rotor. The vibrating cabin lurched forward and soared into the air. Tanapat gripped the clipboard. "Don't we take off only after the checklist?"

"Whatever!" The general replied. He held a microphone to his mouth.

"Ground, this is Condor, I have clearance. Winds zero- two -zero at five. Altimeter three -zero decimal one- zero. I have an India- Delta- India- Oscar- Tango -on board, please advise." Even with no technical knowledge, Tanapat had worked out that the radio microphone was not connected. However, he'd been slow to work out that; 'India- Delta- India- Oscar- Tango' was the word 'idiot'.

"What yo' mama and papa say about this, you being MIA boy?"

"Say again," Tanapat, shouted back.

"Don't get flaky on me boy. What yo' Ma and Pa say about you taking a ride in this here helicopter?"

The helicopter abruptly banked to the right, pushing Tanapat's sweating face into the side window. The general shouted even louder over the blare from the engine and rotors.

"This is the deal, kid; you get twenty minutes T.O.T., Time on Target. We can even fly over your hooch if ya wanna."

The general reached down to his left onto the floor. He struggled to grasp a piece of paper with his thick padded gloves. He stretched out the small piece of paper over his shoulder.

"This is for you boy. That Mandrake dude said I should give it to you when we're up." Tanapat grabbed clumsily at the paper between his gloved fingers.

"That Mandrake fella was sweating like a fat man on a trampoline when he wrote that note. Sick as a dog he was. Kept looking up, thought he was prayin' or something. Wouldn't talk, wouldn't read the checklist, wouldn't even wear the gloves, meaner than a dog on a meat truck."

Tanapat read the handwritten note. It simply said, 'Don't look up."

Tanapat immediately looked up and put the paper in his jacket's inside pocket. What was he supposed to be looking for? After a few minutes, Tanapat had to cover his eyes with one arm. The general saw what he was doing.

"Wouldn't do that if I were you, boy."

Tanapat mumbled to himself, "What did Mr. Mandrake want him to see?"

The general laughed. "Looking at the sun through them rotors, it'll make you toss ya cookies.

"Do what?"

"…yak attack, Technicolor yawn, pray to the porcelain goddess, get sick boy, it'll make you throw up. As I always suspected, that damn Internet has killed the art of conversation."

The small helicopter, with its whirring and beating rotors, swooped over Pastor Jack Lovetree's Baptist Church like an avenging angel. The general plunged to Lakota Street East and over the town's only carpet shop, 'Carpets People Can Walk On'. He hovered like a menacing insect over Jed I. Knights, Mini Mart, and finally climbed back into the blue sky, over the top of the Crazy Horse Bar and Grill and the roof of the Mona Pizza restaurant. For twenty minutes, Tanapat peered above, to the left and right, down at the town, looking for some clue, some reason why Mr. Mandrake wanted him to make this journey.

As the helicopter finally spiralled, hovered, and landed near the general's trailer, not at all disguised from the air by the camouflage netting, Tanapat scanned the inside of the cabin and down onto the deck for any hint or suggestion about what Mr. Mandrake wanted him to discover. He tried to look up again for a few minutes, but it was painful in his eyes.

Back on the ground, with the rotors still spinning, the general jumped out into a fog of ground dust, removed his helmet and gloves, and spat.

Tanapat staggered out of the door, feeling dizzy, and leaned heavily against the helicopter for support. Alarmingly, the general spun around and marched back to him. He glared into the boy's face and narrowed his bloodshot eyes. Tanapat stood at attention but didn't know why.

"We soldiers...," the general growled. "We soldiers can do nothing but destroy God's creation. That's what we do. We kill! War is bad. If they ask you to go, boy, you tell 'em, Hell NO! You don't go. Now give it to me."

Tanapat was terrified. "What... give? Give what?"

"The gloves dumbass, maybe you ought to sit boy, you look nauseous."

Tanapat peeled the gloves off and gave them back to the general.

"Y'all come back now. Tell your friends." The general strutted off and disappeared into his trailer, tripping over the two steps.

"Insane," Tanapat concluded as he watched the general troop away.

"He said nauseous," Tanapat repeated, "...nauseous...nauseous..."

He pulled out his cell phone and displayed the photos of Mr. Mandrake's house. He flicked eagerly through the images and stopped at one particular picture; it was the image of Mandrake's living room. He noticed something at the top of the photograph; he hadn't bothered to see before.

"SO, THAT'S HOW YOU DID IT!"

He observed closer at the detail in the image. He could make out the shadows on the living room ceiling from the blades of a ceiling fan. Tanapat had still not recovered from the frightening flight. He had never experienced fear like that in his life. It reminded him of another time, of fear, anxiety, and horror, a near-death experience. As he staggered away from the helicopter, he recalled that terrible and terrifying day when - he could hardly bring himself to recall it - , the day the Internet went down!

Tanapat was focused on the photograph of Mandrake's living room. In the picture, at the top of the wall near the ceiling, he could now see the blurred shadows of two blades from a ceiling fan. If it was true and his theory was correct, he now knew what Mr. Mandrake had done to his wife. He had to get back home. He had to do research. Beads of perspiration dripped down his forehead. But it wasn't the general's suicidal sprint around the town of Spoons causing his anxiety.

It was the final awareness, the total acknowledgement that this was no longer a teenager's game. Mr. Mandrake had killed his wife and he and Heng were the only ones who knew. That evening, the parents of both boys were shocked and astonished at their sons' sudden, unexplainable, and rather disturbing new interest in doing homework. Neither of the boys would leave their bedrooms until their work was completed.

Chapter Nineteen

Tanapat stood in front of the Mandrake house that Thursday evening after school. It had been easy to find, being the only house in the street wrapped in crime scene tape. Heng was already at the front door, waiting.

"Take them off!" Tanapat ordered.

"But everyone wears sunglasses at a crime scene." Heng protested.

"What the hell are you wearing?"

Heng had draped himself, from head to foot, in a white plastic raincoat, with a plastic hood and plastic booties, covering his baseball shoes. "Crime scene investigation body suit," Heng spun around so Tanapat could get the full effect.

"Off!" Tanapat walked around the house to the back door. Heng followed, shedding his plastic skin, rolling it into a tight ball, and packing it away in his backpack.

Tanapat stopped. "Heng, why are you wearing no shirt?" He didn't want to know.

"Any man stripped to the waste in the movies never gets shot, everyone knows that."

It was difficult, but Tanapat tried to ignore him. He looked about before opening the back door into the kitchen. Heng gripped his arm tightly. "Wait, Boss, are you shining me? There might be a bomb fitted with an electronic timing device with a large red readout."

Tanapat reached for the door handle. Heng offered Tanapat a paperclip.

"What's that for?"Tanapat reluctantly enquired.

"In the movies, any lock can be picked by a credit card or a paper clip."

Tanapat turned the handle and opened the door to the kitchen. "Behave."

"When do we visit the strip club?" Heng grinned. "The two cops always get to visit a strip club in crime movies!" Heng mumbled resentfully and produced a flashlight.

"What are you doing now?"

Heng was astonished. "We need to see what we're doing."

"Turn the kitchen light on."

Heng was genuinely shocked. "You never turn the lights on, at a crime scene."

Tanapat turned on the lights. Heng moved forward. "I'll check the ventilation shafts."

"What the hell are you talking about now?" Tanapat snapped angrily.

"It's a house, not a submarine, there is no ventilation system." Heng sniffed the air. "I can smell chloroform."

"No, you can't."

Heng started to open kitchen cupboards and drawers. "We need to find Mandrake's scrapbook of old newspaper clippings. They always keep souvenirs of their crimes."

"JUST STOP!" Tanapat demanded.

Heng looked at the floor. "I'm sorry! You see it all started when I was six years old….."

"What?'

Heng sighed, "…in the movies, the cop always confronts his past problems at the crime scene."

Heng opened the fridge. "No milk!" he recorded.

Tanapat pushed open the door to the living room. "Wait until you get home if you want to drink something."

"No milk may be a problem," Heng whispered to himself, "but I suppose it wasn't going to be that easy."

They both entered the darkened living room. Heng headed for the light switch.

"NO! Leave it off." Tanapat barked.

Heng shrugged indifferently and paced around the room.

Tanapat checked the first photograph of the living room on his cellphone. He needed to restore the room to its original state before his father entered the house. He opened the curtains and moved the armchair back in front of the window. The room was now illuminated in the evening light and Heng headed for the movie collection, but there was nothing of interest: Star Trek, a war documentary, The Sound of Music, 'Electrical Wiring for Beginners' and DVDs about criminal trials. However, the thin book squeezed in between two of the DVD cases, 'Clinical Paramedic Procedures' was of immediate interest.

Heng sat on the armchair, crossed his legs, and started to flick over pages, first looking at the diagrams and captions. Tanapat looked at the position of furniture and fittings.

"According to my dad, Mrs. Mandrake went shopping every Wednesday at 11 am."

Heng paid no attention to this less-than-startling revelation.

"My dad stopped her going and she returned to the house. Mandrake knew my dad would not let her go shopping. So, what did Mrs. Mandrake do?"

Heng didn't care.

"She couldn't follow her normal routine, so she did what she always does when she has time on her hands. Mr. Mandrake knew this. She sat on that armchair and resumed her knitting."

Heng had now stopped wildly flicking over pages and was reading one page of 'Paramedic Procedures' with growing enthusiasm.

"My dad came in and checked on her." Tanapat continued. "He saw she was sitting in front of an open window, so what does a good police officer do?"

"Makes her sign a false confession?" Heng offered sarcastically.

"My dad moved the chair away from the window and closed the curtain. Mrs. Mandrake turned on the light and ceiling fan. Exactly what Mandrake had planned."

Tanapat dragged the armchair, with Heng still in it, to the new position identified in the second photograph of the living room.

"My dad closed the curtains."

The room was plunged into darkness.

Heng protested, "OK, Sherlock, what does this prove?"

Tanapat turned on the ceiling fan and light. The blades of the fan started to churn the air and whirr like the wings of a large moth.

"Mr. Mandrake knew what his wife would do and exactly where and when she would be doing it…"

"So?" Heng rolled his eyes.

"Mandrake made his wife sick by using flicker vertigo," Tanapat announced, pointing at the ceiling fan. Heng put the book on his lap. "Flicker what?"

Tanapat stood by the light switch on the wall and searched his pocket for his Army knife. He had done his homework and had come prepared.

"It started a long time ago with some helicopter accidents…"

Heng looked up at the dim light bulb and the rotating blades of the fan.

"…A Euro-copter passenger service went down in France in 1979, killing five passengers, then a police helicopter struck a power line in Missouri in 1988 and two people died. Investigators discovered in both cases the helicopter's main rotor blade spun at 105 revolutions per minute, which was the cause. The sunlight shining through the rotor blades caused a flicker like a strobe light.

After a couple of hours, this flashing light caused an imbalance in brain-cell activity, headaches, dizziness, and nausea. They called it the 'Critical Flicker Frequency' or 'Flicker Vertigo'.

All helicopter engines had to be re-calibrated, by law, to make the blades rotate at a higher frequency, 120 revolutions per minute, then the human visual system sees the light as continuous, not as a flicker. For the blades on a simple ceiling fan, with a living room light bulb, smaller blades, and a dimmer light, you would have to experiment with the voltage."

Tanapat noticed the paint, which had once covered the screw heads in the plastic casing of the light switch, had recently been scratched away. He extended the small screwdriver on his army knife and started to remove the screws.

"My dad said Mr. Mandrake was the one sick for a couple of months before the arrest. Don't you see? He was experimenting on himself. He would first have to lower the electrical current to the fan from this wall switch. The rule is thick wire higher current, thin wire, lower current. He would have to change the standard 12 gauge wires in the light switch to 20 gauge thin wire and extend their length. There is more resistance in the thin wire. The thinner and longer the wire, the lower the current, the lower the current dimmer the light, and the fan blades rotate more slowly when it's turned on."

He released the final screw and the plastic case fell easily away into his hand. Inside a contorted jumble of wires, too much wire to fit comfortably they started to uncurl, undulate and unravel like worms. It was soon clear, that someone had added longer thinner wires to the original wiring.

"Over a couple of months, in Mandrake's late-night experiments, he had worked out the speed of the blade rotation to achieve critical flicker frequency and how long his wife would have to be exposed to the effects of the flickering light before she started to feel physically sick. The light bulb is dimmer, and in a dark hot room with the curtains closed, the fan blades are made to rotate slower than normal by changing the electrical current, and Mrs. Mandrake is under stress and concentrating hard on her knitting.

Remember what Pamela said? Intarsia knitting stitch would need a lot of concentration. After two hours, Mrs. Mandrake feels sick enough to want to go to the bathroom. She did exactly what Mandrake wanted and when he wanted her to do it. He didn't have to be here to make it happen."

Heng snapped the book shut melodramatically and threw it to Tanapat, who caught it just in time. Heng first stood and then marched purposefully. "Exactly right dude!" Heng said excitedly, as he left the room.

Tanapat followed him holding the book. Heng checked the bathroom shelves for the necessary ingredients to confirm his new theory. He lifted the toilet cistern lid and placed it on the floor. He reached into his trouser pocket and pulled out a small plastic container, carefully unscrewing the cap. He produced a large white oily pellet. Tanapat giggled.

"We have been through this before Heng. It didn't work remember?"

Heng once again balanced the pellet on the float ball inside the toilet tank.

"I too have been doing my homework! This is what Mandrake did before he left for the Police Department, in the morning, to establish his perfect alibi, getting himself arrested by your dad.

As you said, Mrs. Mandrake came in here to be sick and put her head over the toilet bowl as people do."

Heng pushed the handle to flush the toilet. The float ball angled upwards pulling the flush chain tight, which opened the flush valve at the bottom of the tank. The oily pellet slid off the ball into the tank of water and the tank began to drain rapidly into the toilet bowl. The pellet floated on top of the water and sank with the water level. There was no reaction from the pellet this time.

Tanapat was puzzled. "I don't understand, what is wrong with the pellet?"

Heng smiled and gently pushed Tanapat back from the toilet, out of harm's way. As the water level reached the bottom of the tank and the water gushed into the toilet bowl, the reaction of the sodium in the pellet began. Once again, it started its frenzied twirling, twisting, and flashing as it expelled small jets of gas propelling the pellet feverishly across the surface of the remaining water in the tank. The water in the toilet bowl started to gently bubble as the gas was released. The pellet fizzled, dissolved, and vanished.

"I made the pellet, hydrophobic, water repellent with water-soluble oil."

He picked up the bottle of Baby Oil from the bathroom shelf he'd noticed when he entered the bathroom, "like Mandrake did, with this oil, probably. Mandrake did what I did. He covered the pellet in water-soluble oil. It slows the reaction of the pellet in water. The oil takes a little time to dissolve, enough time to delay the reaction and start later, nearer the water valve at the bottom of the tank, releasing most of the gas into the toilet bowl. If Mrs. Mandrake was leaning her head over the bowl, trying to be sick, breathing heavily, she would have inhaled nearly all the gas."

"It's brilliant Heng! Mrs. Mandrake breathed in the gas. But you said it wasn't poisonous."

"It's not," Heng confirmed.

"Well?" Tanapat asked thinking the whole demonstration was a waste of time.

"Not poisonous on its own, but Poly-Sodium-Benzdioxin is a reactant. If you mix it with another chemical, there is a strong reaction, a fatal reaction. That's why they stopped using it as bleach in paper mills, it's why they banned the compound."

141

Tanapat became interested. "Mixed with what?"

Heng nodded to the book Tanapat was still holding, "page 23, at the bottom. Mandrake had also done his homework."

Tanapat impatiently flipped over the pages. Heng now looked at his watch.

"A strange book for an English teacher to have, don't you think?" Heng observed pretentiously. "Old Man Rivers said a short time after exposure to the Poly-Sodium-Benzdioxin gas, the workers who had died in the paper mill, had been drinking milk. Milk is a complex biological fluid with seven main components: water, fat, protein, lactose, minerals, vitamins, and enzymes but by far the biggest ingredient is lactose."

Tanapat had found the page and now started to read the small paragraph at the bottom. "The standard paramedic procedure for any patient..." he quoted, "... with presenting symptoms of chronic nausea and vomiting, always check blood pressure, heart activity, pulse, and level of consciousness are normal. Then an I.V. drip of Ringer's Solution with 25 milligrams of Phenergan. A nasal cannula for oxygen, at two litres per minute, is optional."

Heng pointed a finger to the smaller text, in the reference, at the bottom edge of the page. "Now look at the main ingredient of Phenergan."

Tanapat read the reference. "The main ingredient of Phenergan is lactose."

"Damn right!" Heng announced.

"Lactose?" Tanapat didn't understand.

142

Heng explained, "The main ingredient of Phenergan is lactose. It's also the main ingredient in milk. Poly-Sodium-Benzdioxin is only toxic when mixed with lactose and only within the first hour of exposure. According to my research, when the Poly-Sodium-Benzdioxin gas, in Mrs. Mandrake's blood, reacted with the Phenergan given by the paramedic in the ambulance, it caused something called Neuroleptic Malignant Syndrome. Looks exactly like a heart attack. Mandrake had timed it all perfectly, where his wife would be, what she would do, and when she would do it. He knew your dad and the ambulance paramedic would follow procedures by the book. He also had a copy of the book they would follow; Mandrake's wife, your dad, the paramedic, and the police department, all puppets on his strings.

"And us as well Heng," Tanapat reminded his friend." He knew we would find out. How do we fit into this? We are his puppets too."

Heng nodded and grinned, He looked at his watch again.

"Very good Mr. Mandrake, very good. Whilst you are locked up in a police cell you know your wife would be forced to stay in a closed, badly lit, hot room, eventually making her sick by a flickering light bulb behind a spinning ceiling fan. The toilet was rigged to release gas when she tried to be sick and the innocent ambulance paramedic made her take Phenergan, with the main ingredient that has a deadly reaction with the gas, all within an hour of her coming into this bathroom.

Mr. Mandrake killed his wife by remote control. The perfect murder!"

Chapter Twenty

The Court House had been built back in the day when the good citizens of Spoons expected more tourist dollars to pay for such grand declarations of municipal pride. The near-empty wood-panelled courtroom now echoed with the malicious prattle of the few spectators, expectantly waiting for proceedings to begin, on this hot and humid Friday morning.

A place at the Mandrake arraignment hearing had become the hottest ticket in town, at least for those few who had followed the gossip.

Mr. Carl Bernstein, Editor of the 'Spoons Bugle', apathetically doodled in his notepad.

Dolores Brunski from 'Shooz', which sold shoes, held a small mirror and applied lipstick like it made a difference.

Wilhelmina Dawkins, who had closed her shop 'Carpets People Can Walk On', was mentally measuring the court's bare floors for carpets.

Pastor Jack Lovetree from the Baptist Church was asleep, dreaming about his favourite sins.

Abner Bracegirdle from the Spoons Savings and Loan Bank rested one arm across his chest, as though swearing the oath of allegiance, but he was guarding the much-reduced check for three million, three hundred thousand dollars in his left inside jacket pocket.

Mr. Norbert Delaney, the manager of the Crazy Horse Bar and Grill, was prodding and poking at the upholstered arms of his chair, reckoning if they would be a worthwhile investment for his Bar and Grill.

Jed I. Knight, known to everyone in town as, 'that no account white trash from the Mini Mart,' was picking at one of his few remaining teeth after eating popcorn from a large noisy, plastic bag.

Mr. Joe Cornfoot, from the Boot Hill Gift shop, was talking to Mrs. Magnolia Macarthur from the Mona Pizza about the sensational and fascinating history of the pizza.

On the front row, Sergeant Wattana sat alone, waiting to give his evidence. And behind the two large, dark, heavy pine tables at the front of the court, sat Bobby Bodean, the ambulance paramedic, Dr. Richard Boyle from the Medical Clinic, and Mr. William Winer III, a lawyer from the District Attorney's Office in the city of Sioux Falls.

At the adjacent table sat the defendant, Mr. Mandrake, with Mr. Ray-Nathan Damon from the Public Defender's Office, also in Sioux Falls.

Rising far above, as Olympian Gods should do, the empty Judge's bench and far below, the Court Clerk's inferior table, next to the Witness Box, a three-sided wooden enclosure.

Buford Tattersall, the judge presiding, entered, unannounced, from one of the two doors positioned on either side of the Judge's bench, catching the clerk off guard. The Clerk of the Court stood quickly.

"All rise for his honour, Judge Buford Tattersall. The people of the state of South Dakota versus Mandrake; arraignment proceedings concerning Criminal Action 0910017 will now be heard before this Court. Counsels will now identify themselves for the record."

Everyone stood, except Jed I. Knight at the back of the court, who had missed the relevant television episodes of 'Law and Order' and didn't know what to do.

The Honorable Buford Tattersall brought down his gavel hard on the wooden block with a suitably intimidating echo that bounced around the cavernous room.

"Y'all be seated." The Judge motioned.

Mr. William Winer III sat down and stood again as if he was on a spring.

"Good morning, Your Honor, William Winer III for the State, U.S. District Attorney's Office, Sioux Falls.

Judge Tattersall arranged his papers and moved the jug of water closer to the glass. "Good morning, Mr. Weener, so entered."

Mr. William Winer III, who had already sat down again, stood again. "It's pronounced 'Viner', Your Honor."

Judge Tattersall removed a gold pen from his jacket's top pocket and pretended to write the correct pronunciation. "So entered."

Mr. Ray-Nathan Damon stood."Good morning, Your Honor. Ray-Nathan Damon, Public Defender's Office representing the defendant."

Judge Tattersall opened the indictment document now passed up to him by the Clerk. "Good morning, so entered. We'll proceed with the arraignment.

Mr. Demon, have you had an opportunity to review the indictment with your client?" "I have, Your Honor." Ray-Nathan Damon rested a friendly hand on Mr. Mandrake's shoulder.

Judge Tattersall nodded in the direction of Mr. Mandrake. "All right, and has he received a copy of the indictment?"

"Yes, Your Honor," the defence confirmed.

"All right then." Judge Tattersall gestured to the Clerk to continue.

The Clerk took a deep breath.

"You are charged, under the South Dakota State's criminal code 564 concerning the said statute that you, Mr. Blake Mandrake, now resident in the town of Spoons, Nuthook County, South Dakota, unlawfully and with malicious criminal intent made a statement whose sole purpose was to indicate an intention to commit grievous violence to your then wife, the late Mrs. Theodora Mandrake."

Jed I. Knight, at the back of the court, laughed out loud. "Wish someone would commit grievous violence to my wife!"

Judge Tattersall craned his neck to see where the interruption was coming from. His eyes found their target. "Is that you, Jed? I swear you're as dumb as a donkey in a ditch. I don't want any of that talk in my court, is that clear?

Jed I. Knight shrugged apathetically, "Yes, judge!"

Judge Tattersall examined his documents.

"...According to the State legislature's amendment of 1996, this statement is criminal intent and a Class B misdemeanour. The range of punishment for this offence is a fine of no less than $500 and not exceeding $2000. Do you understand the allegation against you and the punishment for this offence?

Mr. Mandrake started to stand, but his attorney pulled him back into his seat. "I do, Your Honor" Mr. Mandrake responded.

"How do you plead, guilty or not guilty?" asked Judge Tattersall indifferently.

Mr. Mandrake looked once at his attorney and the Judge. "Guilty," He replied.

147

Jed I. Knight shouted. "GET A ROPE!"

Judge Tattersall banged the gavel. "Jed, I won't warn you again!" He pointed the gavel at the Defense Attorney.

"Mr. Demon...." The judge was immediately interrupted. "...Damon, it's pronounced Day-Mon, Your Honor."

Judge Tattersall ignored him.

"...In your deposition, Mr. Day-Mon, on behalf of your client, you indicate he had been warned of his rights at the time of his arrest and he understood all of the warnings given to him at that time. Does your client wish to have his rights explained again at this time?"

Mr. Ray-Nathan Damon nodded, "No, Your Honor."

Judge Tattersall was doubtful. "Your deposition indicates your client has waived his right to trial. Is it still your client's intention to proceed without further rights to a trial?"

Mr. Damon nodded, "It is, Your Honor, nolo contendere."

Judge Tattersall inclined one ear toward Mr..Damon,

"What?"

Mr..Damon sneered, "No contest, Your Honor, nolo contendere,"

Judge Tattersall drank some water.

"I see! Now let's be clear, Mr. Mandrake. Have you had an opportunity to talk with your attorney about this?"

"I have, Your Honor." Mr. Mandrake responded.

Judge Tattersall was still unconvinced.

" Now, I'm sure you are an intelligent man, Mr. Mandrake. Has your attorney explained the consequences of a plea of guilty or no contest? You have waived your right to a trial before a jury and waived your right to call witnesses to testify on your behalf. Do you understand you are giving up your right to question the State's witnesses and the chance to present your witnesses, the right to cross-examine your accusers? Do you understand you are giving up your right to remain silent?"

Mr. Mandrake knew the procedures, in detail, "I understand, Your Honor."

Judge Tattersall shrugged.

"I see, very well! This court will assess punishment upon evidence, at the court's discretion. You have pleaded guilty or no contest and this will result in a final conviction today on the charge? Do you understand what I just explained to you?"

"I do Your Honor."

Judge Tattersall looked directly at Mr. Mandrake's expressionless face.

"The State's attorneys can proceed. Mr. Weener..."

Mr. Winer stood and looked across at Mr. Mandrake.

"Thank you, Your Honor. We intend to offer into evidence the statements of the first responders, the paramedic attending Mrs. Mandrake, and the doctor at the Medical Clinic."

Mr. Damon threw up his hands in surprise.

"Objection, that is irrelevant, Your Honor. My client isn't being arraigned on a felony. What possible bearing do the paramedic and doctor's statements have in this case?"

Judge Tattersall gave a gentle tap with the gavel. "May I remind you Mr. Demon...?"

"That's Day-Mon..." Mr. Damon rolled his eyes,

Judge Tattersall continued. "...your client has waived his right to both a preliminary hearing and a trial! The State's Attorney can introduce any evidence or expert testimony he chooses at this arraignment. However, I also warn the State's Attorney not to waste the court's time and remember the defendant has been charged with a misdemeanour and has already pleaded guilty."

Mr. Winer insisted. "I appreciate that Your Honor, but I would still like to introduce these statements as background for the record."

Judge Tattersall sighed heavily. "Very well, whatever cranks your tractor, boy, make it brief. Objection overruled, proceed."

Jed I. Knight clapped enthusiastically from the back. "Like T.V. ain't it? Them two city slickers. Don't need no fancy lawyers to tell me he's guilty. He said he was gonna do his wife and his wife got done. It's simple, you plant a tater, you get a tater."

Judge Tattersall erupted. "JED, I WILL HAVE YOU REMOVED!"

Jed I. Knight looked around innocently at the other spectators.

"Don't throw me out, Judge. Look, I got all gussied up special. I ain't botherin' y'all."

"LAST WARNING, JED!" Judge Tattersall waved a hand. "Mr. Weener..."

"...Winer..."

"Yes."

"In the defendant's confession...."

Mr. Damon raised his hand. "Objection, Your Honor! The corpus delicti rule provides that a confession isn't enough for a conviction..."

Mr. Winer interrupted. "...Your Honor, there is nothing in the indictment that bars the admission of any confession given voluntarily or any self-incriminating statement. People versus Moore, 1966..."

"...Your Honor, there was no actusreus." Mr. Damon complained.

Jed I. Knight whispered to nobody in particular. "They talk real pretty, don't they?"

Judge Tattersall gestured to both. "Counsels will approach."

The two men walked over to the Judge's bench, reluctantly, like naughty children expecting detention. Judge Tattersall leaned over from his bench.

"I don't want any of that big city law firm talk in my court. We'll have plain speakin' for plain folk."

Mr. Mandrake had loaded his lawyer for this eventuality. Mr. Damon persisted.

"Your Honor, to establish criminal intent you must unite the statement with the act before you can call it a confession. People versus Mendoza 1997 and People versus Lopez 1999."

Judge Tattersall grinned. "Come on! The man said he was gonna kill his damn wife. He wrote it down, in front of witnesses. He said he was gonna kill her. You know it, I know it, he knows it. It's a confession! But this ain't no murder trial! He's only being charged with the statement of criminal intent."

Jed I. Knight tapped the shoulder of Mr. Delaney, on the seat in front. "I haven't had this much fun since my Papi died."

Mr. Winer flipped papers on his clipboard, which, to the judge's dismay, seemed to hold many, many such papers. "Your Honor, I would like to call one of the first responders at the scene, to give evidence at this time, the paramedic in the ambulance."

The judge sighed and looked at his watch, "Very well, if you must."

Bobby Bodean ambled forward nervously. The Clerk of the Court swore him in. Mr. Winer, at first, spoke in a strange soft tone making Bobby Bodean and all the spectators frightened.

"Now Bobby, tell us what happened, in your own words. You arrived at the Mandrake home fifteen minutes after getting the call from Sergeant Wattana, is that correct?" Bobby looked at the judge for permission to speak.

"Yes sir, ten to fifteen minutes, it was about that time."

"You entered the house?"

"No sir, Mrs. Mandrake was escorted to the ambulance by Sergeant Wattana."

"And the Sergeant told you Mrs. Mandrake had been nauseous and may have wanted to vomit, correct?"

"Yes, sir."

"Did he tell you there were suspicious circumstances concerning this sudden illness?"

"Objection!" Mr. Damon stood quickly. "Suspicious circumstances? Sudden illness? Your Honor!"

The judge pointed an accusing pen at Mr. Winer. "Objection sustained, there is no evidence being presented today for suspicious circumstances or sudden illness. The witness need not answer." Mr. Winer impatiently turned over five more pages on his clipboard.

"Do you have many friends, Mr. Bodean?"

"No, I am married."

Everyone giggled.

Mr., Damon sighed. "Your Honor, what has this got to do with it?"

"I am trying to establish if the witness discussed the case with anyone." Mr. Winer looked disapprovingly at Mr. Damon.

The judge yawned. "Can we move on, boys?"

"Now, what is the usual paramedic procedure when a patient is nauseous or vomiting?"

Bobby responded immediately. "ABC!"

The judge interrupted. "What?"

Bobby smirked. "Check the airway, breathing, and circulation."

The judge made a note. "I'm obliged…"

Bobby continued. "…Then oxygen… "

"THAT IS - A.B.C.O -CAN'T YOU SPELL, DUMBASS?" Jed shouted, trying to be helpful.

Bobby continued. "Then, if we need to, we can give oxygen with a nasal cannula at two litres per minute."

The Judge interrupted, "canula?"

"Sorry judge…a tube,…" Bobby explained.

The Judge made a careful note of the word, 'cannula', always on the lookout for useful alternative vocabulary for his morning crossword puzzle.

"…I administered Ringer's, an I.V. of a sterile solution of calcium, potassium chloride, and sodium chloride in water to treat dehydration and replace electrolytes."

Mr. Winer flicked another page. "And what was the amount?"

"125 millilitres an hour, and I put a cool cloth on her forehead."

"And then what did you do?"

"Because she had recently tried to vomit, I administered Phenergan at 25 milligrams through the I.V."

Mr. Winer looked back at the spectators as though addressing a jury, raising his voice. "And is this the usual procedure for such cases?"

"Oh yes sir, by the book, Ringer's Solution and Phenergan."

"Was Each I.V. bag properly labelled with the time, date, and initials?

"Yes, sir."

"And what happened then? Did you notice anything unusual? Was Mrs. Mandrake in distress?"

Mr. Damon didn't need to even raise his voice. "Distress? Your Honor!"

"Objection sustained," was the drowsy reply.

Mr. Winer tossed over three more clipboard pages. "Did you at any time contact the doctor, at the Medical Center, about any problems?"

"Not at that time. Mrs. Mandrake was awake and everything was normal. Then it happened."

Mr. Winer looked back at the spectators. "Please be as precise as you can. What happened?"

"She arrested!"

Jed I. Knight was angry, "WHY WAS SHE ARRESTED? THEY'RE TRYING TO FRAME MANDRAKE'S WIFE!" he shouted.

Mr. Winer explained. "…That is to say, she had a heart attack, a cardiac arrest, Your Honor?"

Mr. Damon was picking dirt from a fingernail with a pen nib, "Objection!"

"Sustained, let the witness explain by himself."

Bobby Bodean was starting to sweat. "Her airway was clear and secure, with no blockages. I'd got I.V. access with no distress, but she went rigid. Her pulse was all over the place. I started CPR. And the Epinephrine…"

The judge opened his mouth, but Mr. Winer spoke instead,

"Epinephrine?"

"A medication used in emergencies to improve breathing, stimulate the heart, raise dropping blood pressure."

The Judge closed his mouth, "I'm obliged."

"Mrs. Mandrake showed evidence of hypoxemia, that is when the oxygen levels in the blood are decreasing rapidly. I administered the second dose of Epinephrine."

Mr. Winer now flipped pages rapidly. "What was her condition at this stage?"

"The Epinephrine had no effect. She went into shock and her heart stopped"

"Did you fibrillate…?

Mr. Winer looked at the judge. "…That is fibrillation of the heart muscle by applying an electric shock across the chest, Your Honor."

The Judge was beginning to hate this man. "Thank you."

Bobby started to remember the panic he had felt back in the ambulance.

"I was about to begin the procedure when her heart started again. You don't fibrillate if the heart starts, but keep monitoring, vital signs, pulse, and level of consciousness. I continued the I.V. and CPR with 100% oxygen. It was just too late. She was dead when we arrived at the Medical Centre."

Mr. Winer dropped his clipboard on the table jubilantly. "Thank you, Bobby, that's all. I would like to call Dr. Richard Boyle."

Mr. Damon half-heartedly stood, "Is all this really necessary, Your Honor?"

The Judge was also becoming drowsy. "Is it necessary Mr. Weener?" the judge pleaded.

"The doctor needs to confirm the paramedic's statement, Your Honor." Mr. Winer insisted.

Judge Tattersall mumbled, "Jerk!"

"Now, Dr. Boyle, by the time you saw Mrs. Mandrake, in your recovery room at the Medical Center, she was dead. Is that correct?"

"Yes."

"You pronounced her 'dead-on-arrival' and noted the time."

"Yes."

"Did you establish the cause of death, at that time?"

"Not at that time. The paramedic informed me of hyperpyrexia, high fever, irregular pulse, and blood pressure. He said he'd observed cardiac arrhythmia, which means irregular heart rhythms, faster, or slower. I noticed that Mrs. Mandrake exhibited evidence of diaphoresis, which is perspiring, and there was muscle rigidity. I concluded there was enough evidence for heart failure."

Mr. Winer changed to an accusing tone. "Sudden heart failure in a woman otherwise healthy. Is that not unusual?"

The doctor fended off the implication.

"I am not sure what you mean by, 'otherwise healthy'. Mrs. Mandrake was a patient of mine for many years. On the few occasions I saw her, apart from mild arthritis in her right hand, she seemed healthy, and that is true. However, it is not statistically unusual for a woman of her age and weight to have a heart attack, and all the evidence did seem to indicate heart failure as the cause of death. I saw many such cases when I worked at Nabisco Memorial Hospital in Sioux Falls."

Mr. Mandrake was amused to notice Tanapat and Heng standing at the main entrance to the court and he smiled to himself. He then whispered back to Mr. Damon. "Nabisco invented aerosol cheese; cheese you can spray from a can. It was very popular, they made a fortune and the city named a hospital after the company."

Mr. Damon stood and straightened his tie. "Your honour, my client has only been charged with making a criminal statement, a misdemeanour. I question the relevance of all this medical testimony. Is the State's Attorney trying to turn this into a murder trial?"

Mr. Mandrake watched as Sergeant Wattana awkwardly tried to navigate over to the court entrance without being noticed. He then observed father and son in an animated discussion. He assumed it was about his son skipping school to get to the court that morning. He watched dispassionately as Sergeant Wattana hurriedly walked over to the Clerk of the Court and whispered. The Clerk stood close to the judge's bench. Judge Tattersall leaned over as the clerk whispered.

Mr. Mandrake nodded toward both boys, graciously acknowledging their achievement in solving his little puzzles.

"Much earlier than I had predicted," he thought.

The Judge looked annoyed and then puzzled. He glanced over toward the two boys, paused, and lifted his gavel, which fell heavily on the wooden block, awakening all the spectators from a nap.

"There will now be a short recess!" the judge growled.

The spectators stared at each other, not knowing what had happened or why proceedings were suspended. The judge motioned to the clerk and pointed in turn at Mr. Winer, Mr. Damon, and the boys. The clerk paced over to Mr. Winer and Mr. Damon, inviting them to join the judge in his private chambers. The clerk escorted Tanapat and Heng a few steps up to the side door, near the judge's bench.

Mr. Mandrake delightfully imagined the forthcoming theatrical spectacle of the two young comic book heroes in the Judge's Chambers, expounding their solutions to a string of clever clues, which, he had to admit, they had skillfully followed and solved. He was further entertained by the thought of the total and complete indifference these revelations would be greeted by the three professional gentlemen.

Chapter Twenty-One

For Judge Tattersall, Mr. Winer, and Mr. Damon, now assembled in Judge's Chambers, the next thirty minutes would prove to be a tiresome experience. Tanapat and Heng were single-minded in their determination to recount their story of mystery, suspense, deception, and murder, including theatrical reconstructions, with occasional plot twists. However, on the positive side, the time did allow Mr. Damon to successfully eject dirt and grease from under all ten of his fingernails with a pen nib.

Mr. Winer, on the other hand, had sent five text messages to his girlfriend, in Sioux Falls, promising a weekend trip to Hawaii, paid for by the expenses from the Mandrake case, and Judge Tattersall had enjoyed his third cup of lemon tea, from a thermos flask, whilst completing his morning crossword.

The boys' tale began, as all low-budget productions do, with a murder. The young heroes are the chosen ones from dysfunctional families, whose parents don't understand them, and who are only pretending to be dorks. It is the story of the peasant boy who turns out to be king. A band of two brothers, where danger has forged a friendship, one streetwise and cool, the other a lonely geek pushed against school lockers.

The villain gets himself captured on purpose, so clever, brilliant, and seemingly indestructible. A villain who kills, not with razors, ice picks, paperweights, meat cleavers, crowbars, duelling pistols, , or chunks of frozen meat, but with a living room ceiling fan.

The police are, of course, useless. The female characters are missing, or play the mother, or are just plain dead, as in Mrs. Mandrake's case.

There's a computer that instantly solves crimes, a cell phone instead of an all-knowing wizard, important clues overheard by accident, a grizzled local old-timer with a tragic past, who drinks too much, and even a helicopter to make sure it gets added to the action genre bookshelves.

After Tanapat and Heng had finished their epic, there was a long silence. Tanapat, with hands still about his own throat after his final dramatic but inaccurate reenactment of Mrs. Mandrake's last moment, paused and looked at Heng. The judge picked up another sugar lump with the sugar tongs, plopped the glistening cube into the steaming tea, and leisurely stirred with a silver spoon.

Mr. Winer was the first to break the awkward quiet.

"I thought the oil-covered pellet was the best part."

Mr. Damon disagreed. "No, the homework clues were particularly creative, I thought."

The Judge tried to be more encouraging. "Anyone who gets in a helicopter with the Mad General deserves, at least, some respect."

Tanapat could not understand why the three men were laughing at them.

"Well, aren't you going to arrest Mandrake for murder?" Tanapat insisted.

The three men looked at each other, trying not to be the first to giggle, but Judge Tattersall had to smile.

"Mr. Winer, if you would be so kind as to explain to our young friends."

He was grateful the judge had finally got his name right.

"Where's the evidence?" Mr. Winer asked the boys.

Tanapat didn't know what to say next. "But…but…"

Mr. Winer rubbed his tired texting eyes. "There is nothing to link Mr. Mandrake directly to his wife's death. No witnesses, no physical evidence, no expert testimony, and the chief suspect had no opportunity."

Mr. Damon loosened his tie.

"Rules of evidence boys. If the evidence doesn't relate to a particular fact, it's inadmissible in court."

Mr. Winer pressed keys on his cellphone to book a flight to Hawaii on the Justfly.com website.

Mr. Damon yawned. "Is the evidence reliable? The credibility of a source used as evidence, in this case, two teenage boys having illegal access to a crime scene."

Heng was becoming angry.

"What about the clues, dudes, that Mr. Mandrake put in our homework?"

Mr. Winer scrolled the phone screen looking for the cheapest flight,

"Irrelevant, immaterial, no logical bearing on the case."

Judge Tattersall plopped in a second sugar lump, "Objection sustained."

Tanapat protested, "He confessed to my dad!"

Mr. Damon covered another yawn with a hand. "Privileged communication, different case, barred from disclosure in a new case unless it supports new physical evidence, which it doesn't."

Judge Tattersall sipped his tea, "Sustained."

Heng moved forward and stood by his friend. "The gas in the pellets, a deadly chemical reactant..."

"Calls for an opinion from a non-expert..." Mr. Winer casually pointed out.

"Sustained." The judge resumed his crossword.

Tanapat raised his voice, "But I heard my dad say..."

"...Hearsay," Mr. Damon smiled.

"...Sustained," the judge said automatically but then laughed as he wrote the word 'Cannula' as the answer to a clue. A seven-letter word for a tube that can be inserted into the body for medical use - in his crossword.

"The Poly-Sodium-Benzdioxin mixed with the medicine in the ambulance?" Heng insisted.

"Speculation," Mr. Winer said flatly.

"Sustained," the judge, mumbled dismissively.

Both boys looked at each other in disbelief, "What about the changed wiring to the ceiling fans?"

"Immaterial," Mr. Damon scrutinized each of his fingernails for any remaining dirt.

"Sustained," the judge muttered.

163

Tanapat pleaded, "But, Judge, you can't let him get away with it!"

The judge looked solemnly and directly at the two boys.

"Evidence. There is no evidence, boys! Evidence that's been properly collected and preserved for examination. Evidence legally obtained with a warrant. You boys have violated the defendant's Fourth Amendment rights, with your clumsy contamination of a potential crime scene with unreasonable searches and seizures. There must be direct evidence linking Mandrake to the death of his wife. There have to be physical exhibits."

Tanapat felt defeated. Once again Mandrake had out-smarted them.

"How amused Mandrake must be," Tanapat frowned, "knowing that while following all his clues, we would destroy the evidence they needed to catch him. That's why he wanted us to follow the clues. He wanted us to find any evidence he may have missed and then contaminate it. He must have known we would do this from the beginning."

Heng also realized that they had been used by Mandrake. "He didn't need to hide anything. He just needed us to follow his trail and contaminate the evidence so it couldn't be used against him in a court."

Tanapat and Heng, with heads, bowed, walked toward the door. Heng turned his head slightly. "Sorry to waste your time, Judge."

All three men, the Judge, and the two attorneys respected what the boys had tried to do. Mr. Winer watched them walking out of the room, looked at the Judge, and shrugged.

"We're sorry, boys, but without trace evidence, fingerprints or biological evidence such as DNA or even some damn handwriting......."

164

Tanapat froze.

Heng was almost out of the door when he stopped and looked back at Tanapat's face.

Tanapat managed a stammering low whisper, "Handwriting! Did you say handwriting?"

He'd almost forgotten! He felt his heart thumping against his ribs, his face flushed as though he'd drunk a hefty slug of Old Man River's Cracker moonshine.

He gradually looked down at his jacket, the jacket he always wore. Heng followed with his own eyes to Tanapat's jacket. Tanapat turned around.

"The general said Mandrake was sweating like a fat man on a trampoline when he wrote it," he said. "Mandrake was as sick as a dog in the helicopter. Wouldn't read the checklist, wouldn't even wear the gloves." He glared at the judge, his eyes wide and shining with excitement.

"Mandrake wrote me a message. The General gave it to me wearing gloves. I was wearing gloves when I put it in my pocket. It's been in my jacket ever since. Mandrake wasn't wearing gloves. It's in Mandrake's handwriting."

He started to reach inside his jacket. Suddenly Mr. Winer jumped and ran toward him gripping Tanapat's arm painfully tight. Tanapat winced, by instinct, moving his head away as though he expected a punch in the face to follow. Mr. Winer, still gripping the boy's arm to keep him from moving, reached out and stretched his fingers.

"Your Honor, the sugar tongs and an envelope, please."

The judge handed over the sugar tongs. Mr. Winer didn't touch them.

"If you please, can you wipe the tongs clean?"

The judge searched his desk. He saw a linen napkin next to the sugar bowl and wiped vigorously. Now, quite sure they were clean, he stretched out and Mr. Winer took them carefully, reaching inside Tanapat's jacket, probing inside. He went deeper and gripped an object, delicately pulling out a small piece of paper.

"An envelope please if you would be so kind."

The judge opened all the drawers in his desk, like pulling out stops on a church organ until he found a clean white envelope. Mr. Winer loosened his grip on Tanapat's arm.

"Please bear witness, gentlemen, I am placing the evidence into the envelope and then sealing the envelope. Please make a note of the date and time." Mr. Damon checked the date and time on his cellphone, whilst admiring his own now spotless fingernails. "It might be possible, Your Honor." Mr. Winer stared into the boy's eyes for any glimmer or sign Tanapat may not be telling the truth.

"Did you say Mandrake was sweating when he wrote this?"

Tanapat nodded. Mr. Winer sealed the envelope.

"Most paper has a fairly porous surface, so it's easy to get prints in those circumstances. We can send this to the Forensic Science laboratory in Sioux Falls. They'll spray the paper with a glue-like chemical and steam it with an electric iron. There should be a bright purple reproduction of the print on the paper. He might even have left behind some DNA from cells from his contact with the paper if he was sweating that much. How many cells would depend on how much sweat?"

Mr. Winer looked at Mr. Damon. "Of course any defense attorney with half a brain, no offense..."

Mr. Damon shrugged. "None taken."

"...could knock holes in all that circumstantial evidence." Mr. Winer concluded.

"He's correct, Judge. Mr. Damon agreed. "Murder in the first degree would be thrown out at the preliminary hearing."

Mr. Winer smiled broadly at Tanapat. "But murder in the second degree might be possible, at the very least suspicion of murder in the second; the accused intentionally causing the death of another person, by conduct which he knew could cause death or serious physical injury..."

"And Mandrake can kiss goodbye to his insurance payout if he is part of an ongoing investigation linked to his wife's death," the judge added.

Mr. Damon shook Tanapat's and Heng's hands. "That would be enough to provide legal grounds for an autopsy to establish the cause of death."

The judge nodded, "So ordered!"

The Judge wafted back into court and sat down at his bench. He bashed the gavel three times on the wooden block and waited a few more minutes for all participants to resume their proper places, stations, and postures, with appropriate courtroom etiquette. Judge Tattersall waved his gavel in Mr. Damon's direction, who then pushed Mr. Mandrake to his feet. The judge clasped his hands together and rested his head on his fingers.

"Mr. Mandrake, you have pleaded guilty to the indictment that, unlawfully and with malicious criminal intent, you did make a statement whose sole purpose was to indicate an intention to commit grievous violence to your then-wife, the late Mrs. Theodora Mandrake. Under the South Dakota State's criminal code 564, this is a Class B misdemeanour. The court fines you $1500. Please pay at the clerk's desk."

The Judge brought his gavel down heavily on the wooden block. There was a groan of disappointment from the spectators. Abner Bracegirdle frowned and retrieved the check from his inside pocket.

The Judge tapped his gavel three more times lightly, almost unnoticed by everyone now preparing to exit the court.

"Sergeant Wattana, please take Mr. Mandrake back into custody."

Mr. Mandrake, who was paying his fine by credit card to the Clerk of the court, supposed he had misheard. "I don't understand. Custody? On what possible charge?"

The Judge smiled down from the bench, as gods may do from time to time,

"Suspicion of murder in the second degree, Mr. Mandrake."

Jed. I Knight could hardly contain his joy and started to shake everyone's hand and slap backs.

Abner Bracegirdle quietly slipped the check back into his pocket and speedily left the courtroom, calculating a possible reward for the cancellation of such a large payout.

Whilst Sergeant Wattana was drawing Mr. Mandrake's hands behind his back and placing him in handcuffs, Mr. Mandrake feverishly looked around the courthouse until his enraged but still, confused gaze met Tanapat's eyes.

168

Tanapat grinned at him and looked up to the ceiling of the courtroom. Mr. Mandrake looked up to see what Tanapat was looking at. A mallard duck perched on the windowsill outside of the courtroom also looked up to see what the boy was looking at. It was one of the several large fans attached to the courtroom ceiling.

Then Mr. Mandrake remembered.

"The note!"

He closed both eyes in recognition and then resignation, as he imagined the image of a small piece of paper with his sweat-soaked handwriting dancing and floating gently like a leaf falling from a tree, and the sun blinking through helicopter rotor blades.

The mallard duck, balanced unsteadily on the windowsill outside of the courtroom, let loose a rump-ripping butt trumpet and fell off the window ledge.

Chapter Twenty-Two

It was Monday morning and Tanapat was suspicious. His father was wearing his best police uniform, the one that he wore for funerals, the one without the Pizza sauce stain, with black pressed trousers and spit-shined shoes. Pinned to the shirt's top pocket, the seven-pointed gold and blue star of the Spoons Police Department with the motto, 'A duty to serve, no sacrifice too small, short or tall, we arrest them all'.

On his sleeve was a badge, and under the embroidered title, 'Spoons PD', the crossed flags of the American 'Stars and Bars' with the flag of the old southern Confederacy.

Even more suspiciously, his father, who usually at this time in the morning would be pecking indifferently at a computer keyboard with a single practised finger, inputting endless numbers from a large stack of traffic citations, was now engaged in conspiratorial whispers on his cell phone, cupping his hand theatrically over the mouthpiece. He needn't have bothered to make such a mystery, as Tanapat was yawning indifferently, reluctantly rising from his chair and walking towards the front entrance of the Police Department.

"STOP!" his father shouted.

Tanapat had never heard his father shout. He could imagine it was the same tone he would use when ordering a suspect to 'step away from the car and put the shotgun on the ground'. Tanapat swung around with military parade precision. His father was smiling, "I will walk you to school this morning."

Tanapat looked around to see if his father was talking to somebody else. His father never walked him to school! His mind raced through the possibilities.

"It can't be because of the time I put the school up for sale on the internet. That was two years ago. Or, maybe it was last year's parents' evening when I removed one letter from the sign in the school hallway, 'Please display your [p]ass to the teacher on duty.'-that's been forgiven, but probably not forgotten. Maybe it was the time when I painted on the Baptist church sign, 'Are you looking for Jesus?' and I added, 'Try Google". I was just trying to be helpful," he remembered with a smirk.

Tanapat and his father walked down Bruce Springsteen Street. A morning mist had settled quietly, and it smelled of pine trees and old dogs, like a boy's aftershave on Prom Night. The sun was shining behind mashed potato clouds. His father's stride was sure and confident as they marched up Main Street, ever closer to school.

They passed by the Spoons Savings and Loan Bank, which was shut, and on past the Town Hall and Courthouse, the site of Tanapat's recent drama. By the time they had reached the Spotted Elk Laundry, which was also closed, Tanapat was feeling apprehensive. He could not work out, even with his newly practised detective skills, why his father was escorting him to school. After they had glimpsed the carpet shop, called 'Carpets People Can Walk On' and on past Jed I. Knights, Mini Mart on the other side of Lakota Street East, Tanapat's imagination had constructed possible, albeit rather silly, explanations for his father's sudden interest in taking him to school. As father and son paced the strangely empty streets, Tanapat daydreamed about an alternative universe.

His favorite theory was that Spoons was a ghost town and strangers became trapped inside for eternity. He imagined that to protect the town from being changed by the outside world, 100 years ago the Baptist Minister had prayed to the devil to protect the town from outside influence. The devil had granted his wish and now all the citizens of Spoons, forbidden to leave, must live forever in an unchanged world of their own. If they tried to leave, they would grow old rapidly and die.

With this promise of immortality came a curse - the number 13. After the first fifty years, the meaning of the curse became clear. On average, all the people in Spoons had only thirteen teeth, were thirteen kilos overweight, had crashed thirteen cars, had killed thirteen animals with their car, had thirteen empty beer cans on the passenger seat, and always ended up with thirteen meters of crime scene tape on their front door.

Tanapat was jolted back to reality by a shocking sight. Across the road was the Little Big Horn Supermarket, owned by the only Native Americans living in Spoons, Mr. and Mrs. Chapawee. It was closed! He had never seen that place closed. Mr. and Mrs. Chapawee, better known to all as Chief Running Tab and Shopping Dear, kept the supermarket open twenty-four hours a day, seven days a week. Tanapat checked the time as he and his dad finally headed up Main Street to Spoons High School, turning off onto Lakota Street West.

He had not noticed his father slowing down behind him, falling further back as he alone now climbed the school steps. Tanapat stood alone in front of the closed double doors of the school entrance.

Then, the doors started to open. Unexpectedly, there was a riot of clapping and shouting from inside. It seemed to Tanapat that the whole town had crowded into the school entrance hallway, squealing, shrieking, whistling, cheering, and whooping. A forest of cell phones shot into the air on outstretched hands, like mushrooms. With cameras flashing, Tanapat walked forward into the cyclone of cheering. He looked back to his father. His father smiled, "I am proud of you, son." He then nodded toward a familiar face in the crowd and Tanapat turned.

172

Pamela was escorting a small-framed but immaculately dressed woman in a dark blue skirt suit and shiny black hair out from the front of the crowd. It was Tanapat's mother, flown over from Thailand during the weekend, an honoured guest of the town. Tanapat's eyes glistened, as he rushed forward. He hugged her and lifted her off her feet.

"I have missed you so much! I have missed you so much!" he stammered repeatedly in Thai, crying. His mother peppered Tanapat's forehead with little kisses.

Mrs. Magnolia Macarthur from the Mona Pizza and Dolores Brunski from 'Shooz', which sold shoes, were at the back of the crowd drinking warm lemonade from two Styrofoam cups.

"Is that his mother?" Dolores asked, spitting the bitter lemonade back into the cup. Magnolia Macarthur grinned, "That's sweet, isn't it?"

Dolores lowered her voice, "My God, the woman's so thin! I wish my hips were that small?" Magnolia Macarthur smirked, "If she swallowed a meatball she would look pregnant." Dolores giggled, "Still I would like to lose at least ten pounds."

"Take off your makeup, that's six pounds to start with!" Magnolia snapped sarcastically. Both women erupted into cackling laughter.

Mr. and Mrs. Lin pushed their son, Heng forward to join his friend Tanapat. Mrs. Lin had insisted Heng wear a suit for the occasion.

"What's up, Boss dude?" Heng said for want of anything better to say.

Tanapat glared at him accusingly. Heng held his hands in the air, protesting his innocence, "They made me swear I wouldn't tell yo man!"

Heng pointed to the far wall of the hall. "Check that out, dude!" Tanapat held his mother's hand tightly and mouthed the words "thank you" to Pamela, who smiled warmly.

On the school notice board, on the 'Hall of Fame', could now be seen two names in large gold lettering atop the previously empty list of honoured alumni: Tanapat Wattana and Huang Lin. He was pleased, but a little surprised, to notice that they had managed to get the gold paint within the lines

He also noticed that Principal Wyatt Nutter had made a small change to the school rules. Directly below, 'Don't make animal noises at the female teachers,' he'd now crossed out, 'No Cellphones in Class' and added, "In honour of Tanapat and Huang, Cellphones may be used in class for important research"

On the Hall of Shame section of the noticeboard was a message to the effect that all Spoons High School detentions for that week had been cancelled for the first time in the school's history. The school trip for that semester had been hurriedly changed to a two-week trip to Bangkok.

The school canteen 'I Am A Snack Bar, Eat Me' had added two special Asian dishes to their calorific apocalypse: one Thai favourite, Tom Yum Gung, a soup with shrimp, mushrooms, tomatoes, lemongrass, and lime leaves, and Peking duck, considered to be one of China's national dishes -or so the canteen manager had read on Google. Peking duck with its thin and crispy skin would be served with pancakes, sweet bean sauce, or mashed garlic, and with 'cheese melt and fries' as an optional extra.

Meanwhile, Mr. Carl Bernstein, editor of the 'Spoons Bugle' was walking around taking photographs, Pastor Jack Lovetree from the Baptist Church was trying to avoid the romantic advances of Wilhelmina Dawkins, who had closed her shop 'Carpets People Can Walk On' for that morning.

Pastor Jack had been forced to seek sanctuary with Mr. Norbert Delaney, manager of the Crazy Horse Bar and Grill.

Pastor Jack turned his back on her. "There's that dreadful Dawkins woman. She is so two-faced." Norbert Delaney looked over Pastor Jack's shoulder at the woman, "Yes, and neither of them pretty," he dryly observed.

"She dyes her hair," Pastor Jack added bitchily.

Norbert Delaney grinned, "Surely not! She's just prematurely orange."

Pastor Jack gripped Norbert's shoulder. "Do you think Mr. Mandrake killed his wife?" Norbert continued to watch Wilhelmina Dawkins approaching like a shark in a feeding frenzy. "Why not! I think of killing my wife all the time."

Pastor Jack was shocked, "Be serious!" Norbert Delaney became very serious. "It's a small town, not many places to hide the body," he added regretfully. Pastor Jack stared at him in righteous disbelief and walked away into the crowd followed by the determined Wilhelmina Dawkins. Norbert shouted back after Pastor Jack.

"What! I just want revenge. Is that so wrong?"

In the meantime, the 'SpellCheckers'-aka 'The Small Peckers'-consisting of Jim Bob -who liked to be called 'P. Diddy'- Billy Ray Pickett -aka. 'Mr. Mumbles'-Kyle Elwood -'Big Drizzle' -and Jolene Delmont -'Road Kill'-had formed a pre-rehearsed line in the middle of the hall. After a toe-tapping signal from Jim Bob, the whole group started to sway from side to side, tapping a beat with their feet. This was their tribute to Tanapat and Heng.

'Fee, fie, foe, fum, you smelled the blood of the Mandrake, man.

We love ya, man, you had the plan.

While we sleepin', our eyes defective, you detectives with the right perspective.

Be our friend we made a mistake, love yo man, like a fat kid wit cake.

We ain't gonna win, coz we ain't right within.

Fresh start from the heart, please forgive our sin,

I know you can hear me, cuz I'm still feelin you,

We wanna wit us, be part of our crew.

Praise yo names respect we payin'

Be in our rap, ya know what am sayin.'

Double our density with yo smart intensity,

never let us slip, coz then we slippin'.

It was terrible of course, almost as painful as the silence that followed. The kind of embarrassing silence you get at a funeral when someone laughs too long.

Tanapat and Heng courteously moved toward the gang and started shaking hands. Mr. Joe Cornfoot from the Boot Hill Gift Shop couldn't stop blinking. Bobby Bodean, the ambulance paramedic, had become hypnotized by the man's flashing eyelids. Joe Cornfoot, still blinking, tried to start a conversation, "Hippo milk is pink." Bobby Bodean still mesmerized by the flickering eyes opened his mouth. "I didn't know that."

Principal Nutter came behind Tanapat and whispered in his ear while passing him a handkerchief to wipe his wet eyes, "What's all this noise?" Principal Nutter then raised one hand to make an announcement. The crowd became quiet, apart from a few giggles.

"We are gathered here today to celebrate and honour the two heroes of our small town of Spoons, Nuthook County, South Dakota - Mr. Tanapat Wattana and Mr. Huang Lin…"

There was an eruption of applause. Mayor Buford Tattersall stepped forward holding two envelopes. The crowd again settled into an expectant silence.

"With the authority vested in me as Mayor of Spoons, it is my honour and privilege to award Mr. Tanapat Wattana and Mr. Huang Lin, these Certificates of Distinguished Service, for bringing honour to our small town through their meritorious contribution and significant public endeavours within the highest traditions of civilian service in these United States...

Also, Tanapat and Mr. and Mrs. Wattana, with your permission, I would like to offer your son, on behalf of the whole townsfolk, the opportunity to apply for, under our sponsorship, dual citizenship of Thailand and the United States of America. We would like to see Tanapat join his friend Huang Lin at Sioux Falls College after they graduate from High School."

Tanapat tried to smile but knew his family could not afford the kind of money required to put him through college in America. He looked back at his father sadly. His father, however, was smiling mischievously with secret knowledge.

Standing on his own, in a gloom of sincerity and looking as lonely as a pine tree in a parking lot was Abner Bracegirdle from the Spoons Savings and Loan Bank. He was pushed reluctantly to the front of the crowd.

He had been puffed and polished especially for the occasion, wearing his 'best church britches', as he wobbled forward, taking a deep breath and clearing his throat – which is what bank managers do when they are about to talk about money.

"It is my honour and pleasure," Abner announced in a squeaky, whiny tone, "on behalf of my bank, to offer as a reward," he started to mumble, "less the usual administrative costs of course…"

"GET ON WITH IT, YOU OLD FART!" shouted Jed I. Knight, known to everyone in town as 'that no account white trash' from the Mini Mart.'

Abner coughed, "…indeed, to offer these checks for a total of $800,000, which are awarded to Mr. Tanapat Wattana and Mr. Huang Lin, as a reward for their apprehension of…."

The applause and screaming drowned out Abner Bracegirdle's tinny voice and he tried to force a smile despite having to place the checks, very reluctantly, into the hands of both boys. The crowd now engulfed Tanapat and Heng, patting them both vigorously on the back.

For the first time in young Huang Lin's life, he looked over at his mother and father and saw them crying with pride. They were relieved that their son was not now going to be a gangster, a criminal, or a homeless person after all. He was going to college with his friend Tanapat to be a doctor or accountant, or so they assumed. But that was another story.

Mr. and Mrs. Chapawee, owners of the Little Big Horn Supermarket, the only Native Americans living in the town and known to the good citizens of Spoons as Chief Running Tab and Shopping Dear, strolled happily past the school, hand in hand, walking their path together.

They had not been invited to the celebration, not because of any malice toward them from the neglectful townsfolk, but just because, like most Native Americans, they were invisible.

Over the years, the good folk had given Mr. and Mrs. Chapawee many less affectionate titles. He was a bloodthirsty tomahawk-throwing redskin warrior. She was a featherhead teepee squaw. They were dirt-worshipping, maize-munching savages. Nowadays, if the town's only Native Americans were ever referred to at all in casual conversation, they were either the spiritually wise storytellers or a sport's team mascot.

Unlike Tanapat and Heng, however, Mr. and Mrs. Chapawee had nothing to prove and nothing to gain from the approval of the good citizens of Spoons. Long before the white folk had ridden their claim wagon into the territory, millennia before, they already had the right to pray, the right to dance, the right to think, dream, teach, and learn. The white man's laws could not give them what they already had. The truth didn't need a law. Of course, the biggest advantage of being invisible was that Mr. and Mrs. Chapawee, unknown to the people of Spoons, had become the richest couple in town. A secret kept because they didn't use the Spoons Savings and Loan bank or the gossipy and crooked services of the bank manager, Abner Bracegirdle.

They had spent many years selling overpriced garbage to the greedy and gullible citizens from their Little Big Horn Supermarket, eventually making enough profit to buy land and a large retirement home in the most exclusive suburb of Sioux Falls. So there was always a slight skip in their step, as they ambled down Main Street toward Boot Hill Gardens, on their way home.

While there is no scientific agreement about whether or not birds feel emotions, bird watchers like to provide evidence of bird feelings, citing their different personalities and behaviours. Some ornithologists even claim birds have moods, from stress and loneliness to joy and excitement.

While the range of emotional expression may be limited, it was obvious that the large mallard duck, a longtime resident of the town of Spoons, Nuthook County South Dakota, was now very happy perching on the back of the wooden bench in Boot Hill Gardens, gulping and digesting the succulent shiny black Pine Beetle it had finally caught. And, if the duck's hard, keratin beak had been made more flexible, it would have twisted and curled into a contented and satisfied smile. Even the distant and unfamiliar boisterous shindig at Spoons High School had not distracted the bird from its purpose, and it was now content to perch and sleep after a meal, as residents do in Spoons.

Then, just as it closed its eyes and its head sank into its neck, it heard a familiar sound from the top of Main Street. The spatter, fizzle, hiss, and sputter of a small engine straining and struggling- 'putt-putt-putt-putt-putt'. Then, as quick as a city minute, a boom-blast, followed by a cloud of suffocating smoke from the exhaust as the old lawn mower lurched and skidded, with a thresh- thump-pock, down the road apace, left past yonder. It was old man Rivers, riding the saddle like Count Drunkula, on his lawn mower. Snot-slinging and swerving from side to side down Main Street, his hands gripping the driving wheel, and he was panting and frothing like a dog under a hot summer porch. He had sorrows by the bucketful and was hollering down the rain, so blind drunk that he couldn't see through a ladder, jugging his Cracker moonshine.

Old man Rivers,

…he gets all weary, and sick of trying, …

…he's tired of living and scared of dying……

…but old man Rivers, …

..he just keeps rolling along.

180

Made in the USA
Columbia, SC
13 October 2024

43246043R00100